"Will You Never Stop Pulling Away From Me?"

Drew's whispering voice held unmistakable pain.

"I—I didn't mean to," Maria admitted brokenly. "I—you make me nervous."

"Do I?"

He reached out to brush back her hair, his hand exquisitely gentle as he smoothed a few strands from her moist temple. Then, with eyes shut tight, he grasped her thick black hair in both hands and carefully began to slide his fingers down the captured mass.

She knew she should protest this enforced intimacy, but her tongue seemed stuck to the roof of her mouth.

A flame smoldered into life in his eyes, and his hands tightened around her hair. He lifted the ends of the rich, silken bounty to his face, inhaling deeply.

"Your hair smells of sunshine and flowers." He smiled through the strands. "Do you smell like this all over?"

Dear Reader:

I can't let February go by without wishing you a Happy Valentine's Day! After all, this is the day that celebrates love and lovers . . . and it's very special to those of us at Silhouette Books. What better way to celebrate this most romantic of holidays than with Silhouette Desire?

Our "Valentine's Day Man" is sexy *Man of the Month* Roe Hunter in Laura Leone's sinfully sensuous tale, *The Black Sheep*. Roe is a man you're not likely to ever forget, and he really meets his match in Gingie, one of our most *unique* heroines.

Also in store for you is a delightful romance by Dixie Browning, *Gus and the Nice Lady*. Ms. Browning's love stories are always so romantic, so delightful . . . you won't want to miss this one!

Rounding out February are books by BJ James (her many fans will be pleased!), Anne Cavaliere, Noelle Berry McCue and Audra Adams. Don't miss any of these wonderful books.

And next month . . . Diana Palmer brings us a new miniseries, *Most Wanted*, revolving around a detective agency. The first book, *The Case of the Mesmerizing Boss*, is also March's *Man of the Month*. I know, you won't be able to wait for it . . . but March will be here before you know it.

And until March, happy reading!

Lucia Macro
Senior Editor

NOELLE BERRY McCUE
MOONLIGHT MIRACLE

SILHOUETTE *Desire*®

Published by Silhouette Books New York

America's Publisher of Contemporary Romance

SILHOUETTE BOOKS
300 East 42nd St., New York, N.Y. 10017

MOONLIGHT MIRACLE

ISBN: 0-373-05694-X

First Silhouette Books printing February 1992

All the characters in this book have no existence
outside the imagination of the author and have
no relation whatsoever to anyone bearing the same
name or names. They are not even distantly
inspired by any individual known or unknown
to the author, and all incidents are pure invention.

® and ™: Trademarks used with authorization.
Trademarks indicated with ® are registered
in the United States Patent and Trademark Office,
the Canada Trade Mark Office and in
other countries.

Printed in the U.S.A.

NOELLE BERRY McCUE,

who helped launch the Silhouette Desire line under the pseudonym Nicole Monet, lives in California. "I've always loved to read," the author says, "and writing has filled a void in me I was never consciously aware of having. It has added depth to my life and a greater awareness and appreciation of the people around me. With every book I write, I hope I am in some small way paying for the pleasure reading has given me over the years. That's why I write romances, because they leave the reader with a positive attitude toward love, life and relationships. When all is said and done, isn't it love for others that gives us the greatest happiness in life?"

For Lucia Macro,
an editor who gives that little bit more—
be it a kind word of encouragement or
a judicious rap on the head—with all my thanks!!!

One

Maria Fairmont was pleased to see so many in attendance. The dinner dance was organized to raise funds to benefit the Family Assistance Center for Emergency Shelter, which she had founded two years ago with the small inheritance left to her by a dear and loving friend. She was a scared, hostile runaway when she had met Thomas Phelps. He had taken her in from the streets and given her the understanding and support of a father, and in return she had given him as much loyalty and admiration as a true daughter would have.

A member of the Hayward Police Department, Tom had spent years of off-duty time actively aiding the homeless. The plight of the street people had been a cause dear to his heart, and founding an organization to provide them with temporary emergency shelter a goal for his retirement years. After leaving the police force, Tom had continued working as a security guard, determined to provide Maria with a college education. By the time she'd graduated from Cal State University with a degree in business management and was in a position to work with him to fulfill his dream, only the dream had remained. Tom had been lost to her, the victim of a massive coronary.

Maria suddenly stiffened her spine and mentally chastised herself for giving way to her feelings in public. Unless her regrettable temper was aroused, she tended to be outwardly reserved and unemotional, her painful childhood having taught her to hide her vulnerability from the world. But she hadn't been able to hide from Tom, nor from the zany, softhearted friend she'd made in high school. Both Tricia Sinclair—now Tricia Everett since her marriage—and Thomas Phelps had penetrated that shield of reserve Maria surrounded herself with, their gentle persistence eventually wearing away her instinctive mistrust.

Two other people who ran a close second in her affections were Charles and Lynette Holcomb, a couple of runaway kids she'd found hiding out in one of her empty apartment units a couple of years ago. She'd petitioned the courts for custody, and they'd lived with her until recently. When Charlie had secured a good job and could accept responsibility for his sister, Maria had remained as co-guardian of Lynette to satisfy the authorities, and the Holcombs had rented an apartment two floors above hers.

But unlike Tom and Tricia, Charlie and Lynette knew very little about her background. She'd told them that in her teens she, also, had tried to escape from an impersonal social welfare system, but they had no true conception of the kind of person she'd once allowed herself to become. She didn't want them to know. The dark memories that haunted her were hers to bear, and only she was aware that establishing FACES in Tom's memory had been both an act of love and a means of reparation.

As Maria glanced around the crowded room, her delicate features softened at the thought of the kick her foster father would have gotten out of all this hoopla. Hayward's mayor and several prominent members of the city council were in attendance. Added to the roster of attendees were representatives from the fire and police departments and some of the city's most influential men and women in business. The meal provided by the hotel had been lavishly praised, and even the speeches had been very well received.

Now they had adjourned en masse to an adjacent lounge, where a five-piece band had been provided for their entertainment. A loud fanfare from an extremely zealous drummer caused her to wince, and twin dimples immediately peeped out beside each corner of her full, sensually curved mouth as she grinned. She was getting old, there was no doubt about it!

Her boss and Tricia's husband, Marcus Everett, often accused her of being over the hill at twenty-six. He and Tom had been friends of many years' standing, and in fact Tom had been one of the first tenants to take up residence in the Hidden Creek Apartment complex she now managed for the Everett Property Management and Development Corporation. After Tom's sudden death, Marc had pulled her from a morass of grief and depression by bullying her into accepting the job. Caring for the Holcomb children had accomplished the rest.

But now Marc was trying to encourage her to begin climbing his corporate ladder. A rather austere, reserved man with ambition ground into every bone in his body, he just couldn't understand her reluctance to leave the secure niche she'd provided for herself. Only Tricia realized that there had been too much insecurity and too many foster homes in Maria's life for her to easily accept change.

It was this unusual ability to empathize that made Tricia such a wonderful psychologist, Maria thought, and why she had been willing to accept such a woefully small salary to work as a counselor for the Family Assistance Center. Tricia's concern for others was an integral part of her personality, just as Marc's overriding need to excel in business was a part of his nature. Which was why, she remembered with a smile, she had been stunned when the two of them had announced their engagement. She hadn't been able to imagine a more unlikely couple to share the bonds of matrimony.

Redirecting her steps to the table she was sharing with Marc and Tricia, a wayward strand of hair tickled Maria's cheek. With an annoyed grimace, she haphazardly tucked it back into place. The thick, waist-length black mass was parted in the middle and pulled into an elegant yet functional French braid. As she continued to skirt the lounge with quick, economical movements, the glittering sparkle of the ankle-length white-sequined gown she wore formed a striking contrast to her dark coloring.

Eyes turned to follow her progress, but she was unaware of their admiring glances. A niggling ache was beginning to assert itself at the base of her skull, more annoying than painful at the moment. Hiding a yawn beneath her hand, she gave her head a rueful shake. A tired flush emphasized her high, elegantly sculpted cheekbones, her creamy olive-complexioned skin tones taking on the hue of a dusky rose.

But when she spotted a certain tuxedo-clad blond watching her from the dance floor, her exhaustion was replaced by a reviving surge of adrenaline. Her heartbeat accelerated with sickening ferocity, and she shivered as a pair of sexy gray eyes swept over her body with penetrating thoroughness. She didn't even realize her feet had stopped moving until someone stumbled into her from behind. As she muttered a distracted apology, her eyes remained glued to Andrew Sinclair, her best friend's brother and the bane of her existence.

As she had a thousand times before, she wondered why he was the one man in the world who could weaken her knees with a single glance. His effect on her was more than the reaction of a woman to a handsome face and a tall, muscular body. From the very beginning there had been an inner force at work between them. Desire, with all its dark, driven urgency, had linked them together regardless of their opposing wills. And they were both opposed to those silken cords of physical attraction that threatened to wrap them together in an inescapable web.

Tricia had gone to live with her brother after their parents were forced to relocate to Arizona for their mother's health, a move that had allowed Tricia to graduate from high school with the rest of her classmates. But a stricter guardian than Drew had never existed, and although she loved him she'd begun to resent his authority. She hadn't been able to twist him around her little finger as she had her mother and father, which had been a good thing in Maria's opinion.

Although she'd never dared admit it to Tricia, she had viewed Andrew Sinclair's protective attitude toward his much younger sister with approval. She'd already seen firsthand the trouble her friend could get into without firm guidance. Tricia had a carefree personality and a headstrong nature, and Maria's own experiences had made her well aware of the dangers that could arise from the younger girl's innocent enthusiasm for life.

So when she first met Drew she'd been impressed with his maturity and self-confidence, and, with shy admiration and growing fascination, her dark eyes had followed every movement he made. If he'd been aware of her schoolgirl crush, he hadn't let on by word or deed. He had treated her with gentle consideration, and she had blossomed beneath his approving smiles. Their mutual love for Tricia had seemed to form a bond between them, and yet a stupid misunderstanding had forever shattered that tentative relationship in its infancy.

Tricia had defied him to go to a party given by one of the wilder, more free-spirited girls at school. Ironically enough, Maria had tried to talk her friend out of attending, which had made the events that followed seem even more terrible than they were. When Drew tracked his sister down and found her in one of Cindy Langston's opulent bathrooms, throwing up most of the alcohol she'd consumed, it was Maria who caught hell.

Drew had always kept Tricia on a pedestal, and he hadn't believed her capable of falling off it without help. As a result, he'd accused Maria of encouraging his sister to lie to him, of undermining her morals and of getting her drunk. All in all he had accused her of entirely too much, and she'd been too shocked and bitter at his scathing denunciation to even bother defending herself.

As a child in a world of indifferent and often carelessly cruel adults, she'd learned her word meant little or nothing against preconceived prejudice. So she'd reacted to that harsh, censorious voice by maintaining a sullen silence, which had only strengthened his revised opinion of her as a wild, rebellious teenager in search of cheap thrills.

The next day Tricia told him the truth, and she'd called Maria to let her know that her brother would be stopping by her place after work to apologize. But bitterness had completely obliterated every iota of common sense she'd possessed at nineteen, she remembered with a sigh. Drew had punctured a heart that had already received too many wounds, and left her bleeding inside. If he wanted to believe the worst of her, she had vowed vengefully, she would really give him something to complain about!

When he arrived she'd been ready for him and had answered the door in the gift one of her more sophisticated school friends had just given her for her birthday. Of flowing black satin and lace, the negligee and gossamer peignoir was the last word in feminine allure. She'd played the sultry little vamp so well Drew had been tight-lipped with fury, his voice harsh when he asked, "Does your guardian approve of you parading around in this kind of thing?"

He was staring holes through her as he spoke, and at the look in his eyes, a surge of excitement nearly paralyzed her vocal chords. When she finally trusted herself to speak, she didn't bother telling him that this had been the one gift she hadn't shown Tom. Tom would have been just as disapproving as Drew, which was a fact her defiant mood had rushed to suppress. Instead she'd tossed her head and murmured, "Tom enjoys seeing me in pretty clothes."

His thickly lashed eyes had narrowed, while conflicting expressions flickered across his face too rapidly for her to assimilate them. "I...understand."

Suddenly his eyes had darkened, the dilating pupils expanding until she could see herself in their reflection. A sensual smile had caused her to catch her breath in bemused fascination, while his gravelly voice shivered along her nerve ends until she felt his essence in every pore on her body.

But there had still been anger behind that smile, and he had pulled her against his hard frame with a suddenness that had stunned her. "A schoolgirl by day— a beautiful temptress by night," he'd whispered against her mouth.

Strong white teeth nipped at her lips, forcing them to part for the sinuous glide of his tongue. "You certainly had me fooled with that shy, demure act of yours, little gypsy," he'd muttered bitterly. "I thought you were off-limits, when all along you've been another man's property. God, how wrong I was about you!"

Later she realized that her behavior that evening had given Drew an erroneous impression of her relationship with Tom, but then all she'd been conscious of were his caressing hands and demanding mouth. She had been shaking with a co-mingling of terror and forbidden delight, and the desire that so suddenly exploded between them had been as shocking as it was unexpected.

A shiver shook her small frame as she recalled the feel of his strong arms as they tightened around her, and the sensual mouth that had left her lips bruised and aching for just a semblance of tenderness. That single, devastating kiss had been more of a punishment than a reward, but that hadn't lessened its impact on her young emotions.

Eventually Drew had pushed her away from him before the situation got entirely out of hand, but she still cringed to remember the disappointment in his eyes as he stormed out of her apartment. Less than four months after that incident, Tricia was installed in a university dorm, and Drew accepted a political appointment in Washington. But before he'd left for D.C., he had visited her one last time. When he'd suggested she leave Tom and let him take care of her instead, she had been enraged at being thought of as a doll to be passed from hand to hand.

But she'd also been tempted to throw common sense to the winds and go with him, she remembered. During his infrequent visits to the Bay Area, she'd managed to maintain a distance between them, but only because Drew was still furious with her for refusing to become his mistress. She'd welcomed his anger. It had shored up her defenses and enabled her to maintain a barrier between them she knew was necessary if she hoped to resist his sensual appeal.

Then Tom died, and the following Christmas she realized how determined Drew still was to make her his mistress. He'd cornered her in Tricia's backyard, and one look into his glittering eyes had caused her to panic. Without pausing to consider possible repercussions, she had begun prattling on about the latest man in her life. It wasn't really a lie, she'd argued with her conscience. Charlie Holcomb did live with her, and she was very fond of her ward.

An earsplitting clash of cymbals jerked her out of the past and into the present with nerve-racking suddenness, and her attention once more focused on the couple still entwined on the dance floor. The enviably tall, slender female clinging to Drew with limpid determination was instantly recognizable, since Delia Lang's flawless face and emerald green eyes were plastered over magazine covers in every supermarket in the country. Leave it to the egotistical Mr. Sinclair to arrive with a national celebrity to enhance his lady-killer reputation, she thought sourly.

Right at that moment the striking redhead glanced up at her escort, frowning slightly when she noticed his attention aimed at someone other than herself. She looked over her shoulder to follow the direction of his wandering gaze, a petulant slant to her mouth as she spotted her competition. Maria felt the woman's eyes slide critically over her strapless gown before she was dismissed with a haughty toss of tumbled red curls.

Well! she thought indignantly. She might not be wearing a designer original, but at least she could breathe. That silver sheath the other woman was poured into was tight enough to cut off all of her blood circulation. With a disdainful sniff, she decided there must be quicker ways to die. As a blond head was pulled down until pursed scarlet lips were able to smear themselves against their masculine counterpart, Maria suddenly considered several rather clever ways to accomplish such a task.

The cedar-paneled lounge was cozily intimate. Globed amber hanging lamps added a soothing ambience to the overall decor, but Maria was gaining little comfort from the lambent glow. She wasn't jealous, she assured herself staunchly. Drew's date for the evening was making a public spectacle of herself, which was the only reason Maria was feeling such a violent surge of distaste for the other woman.

It was sickening to see a well-known member of her sex publicly fawning over any man, even if he was a big-shot defense attorney who could boast a former U.S. senator for a father. Since his return home he had quickly regained his media popularity, but being the darling of the six-o'clock news didn't make his lady friend's behavior any more palatable. In fact, quite the opposite. The woman was obviously a man-eater with an eye to the main chance, she decided, and if a certain golden-haired lawyer wasn't careful, he was going to be caught providing the main course.

The vengefulness of her thoughts shocked her into averting her gaze, and as her feet regained their former momentum she took several deep breaths to try to attain control of her temper. Fortunately, she had arrived at her table and she quickly seated herself beside a slender, elegantly coiffed blonde with a regal bearing and gentle blue eyes. Leaning sideways, Maria scowled horribly and rasped, "What in the devil is he doing here?"

Tricia Everett took one look at her friend's face and didn't have to search the crowd to know it was her brother to whom Maria was referring. With a shrug of a chiffon-draped shoulder and a slightly caustic glance, she mentioned the task she'd been given in regards to the evening's festivities. "You knew I didn't want you to nominate me again as chairwoman of the invitation committee, but you went right along and did it anyway," she reminded Maria resentfully. "I couldn't very well leave a member of my own family off the guest list, could I?"

"Yes," Maria interjected forcefully.

Tricia clicked her tongue in reproval. "I felt too guilty to refuse, and as a result I had to spend hours on the phone, sweet-talking every well-heeled resident of Hayward into attending this affair. If you hadn't tricked me, you could have crossed Drew off the list yourself!"

Maria's responding glare held not a smidgeon of repentance. "Can I help it if you have a golden tongue, as well as a positive genius for convincing people to do things they don't want to do?"

The other woman snorted inelegantly. "Hmph, if I'm the apple then you're the darned tree. Ever since you used your inheritance from Tom to found FACES, I've gotten stuck with all the dirty work. I simply have no backbone where you're concerned."

"Maybe not, but you do have the necessary social contacts," Maria argued mulishly. "Having been named for the county hospital where I was born, I certainly don't have the same clout as the wife of one of the wealthiest men in the state."

"There you go with that inferiority complex of yours," Tricia complained with familiar disapproval. "I swear that's why you're so paranoid where Drew is concerned. You never felt intimidated by me, but my dear brother makes you prickle like a porcupine. Might I remind you that he's not the monster you imagine him to be, but a human being like the rest of us?"

"That's a matter of opinion!"

Tricia's mouth firmed, her patience wearing thin as she studied the woman at her side. "You have to be the stubbornest person alive, which is probably why I give in to you so often. Surrender is one way of keeping the peace."

Feeling a sudden need to change the subject, Maria glanced around the crowded room. "Where's Marc?"

Tricia's reply held a faintly bitter inflection. "He's with Councilman Davies discussing the new zoning restrictions on that latest property he bought. You didn't think he accompanied me here tonight for mere pleasure, did you?"

Startled by the unaccustomed cynicism in Tricia's voice, she whispered, "Oh, Trish. I hate seeing you so unhappy. If I hadn't introduced you and Marc, you..."

"For heaven's sake, don't you start feeling guilty," Tricia muttered. "You did your best to talk me out of leaping headfirst into marriage, but I was too starry-eyed to listen."

A harsh burst of laughter erupted from her throat, and she grimaced ruefully. "I thought once we were married Marc would devote more time to our relationship. Instead I see even less of him than I did before, and all I've learned how to do is give in to him. But one of these days, I'm going to really rattle that man's bones. Now, enough about my problems," Tricia said hastily, forcing a more cheerful note into her voice. "You and Drew are much more interesting gossip fodder."

"I hope you know he's ruined my evening."

Sudden amusement obliterated the last of Tricia's moodiness, and sparkling blue eyes immediately clashed with a pair of accusing black. "I invited Drew to get at his wallet, not to cause trouble for you, Maria."

"You don't have to try to cause trouble," Maria retorted with a long-suffering sigh, "it follows you around like a shadow."

Although Tricia smiled, her expression suddenly turned serious. "Does Drew's presence here really upset you that much?"

"You know we fight whenever we're together," she countered evasively.

"Yes, and I know why," Tricia retorted. "You've always taken a perverse delight in making him think the worst of you. Every time I've tried to convince him he's wrong, you've done or said something outrageous enough to infuriate him all over again."

"I'm trying to give the dratted man an ulcer."

"You're trying to keep him at a distance, because you've convinced yourself you're not good enough for him."

Wincing visibly, Maria lowered her eyes to the white linen cloth draping the table. "And you know it's true, Tricia."

"I know that what happened in your youth shouldn't be allowed to influence your future." Tricia hesitated briefly and murmured, "You're worthy of being loved, Maria."

"What Drew wants from me isn't love."

"That's your fault," Tricia insisted impatiently. "If you'd only stop pretending to be something you're not, Drew wouldn't treat you the way he does. Don't you think you've carried on this deception long enough?"

"I'm already too vulnerable, Tricia," she whispered with painful honesty. "My powers of resistance are nil, but as long as he believes I'm involved with some man or other, he'll leave me alone."

"Tom is gone," Tricia murmured softly, "besides which, he was your guardian—nothing more. And as soon as Drew gets a look at young Charlie he's going to know you lied about your relationship with him. What are you going to do then?"

"Hide out in the hills." Maria's muttered reply was accompanied by a hopeful look. "Maybe he won't meet Charlie, now that he and Lynette have their own place."

"Don't bet on it, and when he does it's not going to take him long to start wondering how many other fibs you've told him. If you want the truth, I'm so sick of this war between you two I'm tempted to tell him myself."

"But you won't?" Maria questioned worriedly.

"What kind of a friend do you think I am?" Tricia asked, her accompanying smile so sweetly innocent Maria frowned in consternation. "But now that Drew is home for good, I'm going to have to be extra careful not to let on that you and Charlie aren't lovers.

"But one of these days," she warned, "my brother is going to realize that your frenetic love life is pure fantasy. When he does you'd better put on a good pair of running shoes, Maria."

Tricia's smug retort gave rise to Maria's suspicions. She was ready to question her friend about any possible plot she might be hatching, but clamped her lips together when she noticed Drew and his date bearing down on them. "Oh, no," she muttered in disgust. "We're about to be visited by the gorgeous duo."

Seconds later Drew pulled out a chair for his companion and appropriated Marc's for himself. As usual, the first words out of his mouth, as he glanced in Maria's direction, sounded accusatory. "I didn't realize you'd founded FACES."

"Why should you?" Maria countered with a shrug. "As I've mentioned a time or two before, you don't know beans about me, Counselor."

"He certainly doesn't," Tricia interjected slyly.

Completely ignoring his sister, Drew draped an arm across the bare, smooth white shoulders of the woman sitting next to him. "I'm sorry, you haven't met Delia Lang yet, have you, Maria?" With studied casualness he performed the introduction, his expression taunting as he slowly slid his hand up and down his date's slender arm.

Her eyes glittering with temper, Maria managed to acknowledge the introduction with a semblance of courtesy. "Pleased to meet you, Ms. Lang. I hope you're enjoying yourself."

The other woman dismissed her with the slightest of nods, her attention completely centered on Drew. In a little-girl voice that made Maria grit her teeth and Tricia choke on her drink, she murmured, "I want to dance, sugar."

"We just did," he replied impatiently.

Delia began to nuzzle his neck, her simpering response ending in a plaintive sigh. "I just can't get enough of being held by you, Drew."

Tricia muffled a giggle, while Maria jumped to her feet with all the grace of a puppet jerked by a master hand. Mumbling some nonsense about needing to use the ladies' room, she made good her escape before she gave in to the temptation to rearrange a certain red-head's perfect features. With a hopeful prayer for deliverance, she stormed across the room as though the devil himself were at her heels.

Two

The angels were definitely working against her, as Maria discovered when she exited the ladies' room. She was barely halfway down the hall when a firm hand descended on her shoulder like the touch of doom. The hand was accompanied by a clipped, masculine voice that sent prickles of alarm throughout her body. "I've had about enough of this cat-and-mouse game, Maria. If you're through playing hide-and-go-seek, I want to talk to you."

With a shrug she dislodged Drew's fingers and turned to face him. "I'm surprised you noticed anything about me," she remarked with icy cynicism. "The last time I looked you appeared quite... adequately entertained."

"Jealous?" he asked, his mocking arrogance making her long to give him a swift kick where it would hurt the most.

Instead she used her expressive eyes to full advantage, which was a safer alternative to physical violence. "Not at all," she declared haughtily. "If you must know, I pity the poor, deluded woman. Although if she chooses to spend an entire evening pandering to your oversize ego, she deserves to look ridiculous!"

At that his brows knit together with all the elemental force of a thundercloud. He was disturbed by her taunt, disturbed by the image she seemed to have of him. Now that he knew about her involvement with FACES, some of the missing puzzle pieces were beginning to slot into place. For the first time, he was seeing a serious side to Maria, one he'd never guessed existed. There had always been inconsistencies in her behavior, he realized, but those hints at a depth of personality had only confused him.

So he had brushed the inconsistencies aside and deliberately blinded himself. He had refused to acknowledge the generosity she showed her friends, or the glimpses of impishness he'd seen in her eyes when she parried his verbal jabs, or the lack of any real malice in her dealings with him. He had thought her a pretty butterfly, but now he was beginning to realize that she was far from being the shallow, pleasure-seeking woman he'd imagined her to be.

Instead she more closely resembled a honeybee, he decided fancifully, sipping nectar from the flowers without realizing how necessary she was to their survival. When she had refused to move to Washington with him, he'd been too bitter and angry to attribute more than the basest motives to her decision, yet now he had cause to wonder. Had she been necessary to

Thomas Phelps's survival, and had that knowledge been what had kept her by his side until his death?

There had never been reason to question Maria's loyalty and tender heart, her protective attitude to Tricia over the years had proven that. He remembered the times his sister had jumped all over him in defense of her best friend, and he could now approve of her loyalty. It was unfortunate that his heart and mind had been closed to the truth, his inner defenses securely bolstered against Maria's devastating feminine appeal.

But she had haunted him for years, he was now able to admit freely. She'd always been different from all the other women who had come and gone in his life, because there had been an element of purity about her as vital as the elements that governed nature. This black-haired gypsy had the power of Eve at her fingertips and didn't even realize her earthy potency. The thought made him uneasy. Such innocence made her extremely dangerous to the human male...and to him in particular!

Resentment showed in his eyes at the realization, and he quickly shook himself free of his darkly introspective mood. "I didn't get you out here to discuss Delia," he said, returning to the topic of their conversation with more harshness in his voice than he'd intended.

Expelling a sigh of exasperation, she asked, "Then what's on your mind?"

Ignoring her question, Drew responded with a question of his own. "What's this my sister's just been telling me?"

Maria resisted the urge to close her eyes and try to sink through the floor. "About what?" she croaked, her throat tightening with dread.

"You know damn good and well what about!"

She studied him with a martyred air. "If I did I wouldn't be asking."

"Tricia seems to think you and your lover boy are about ready to announce your engagement."

While Maria mentally vowed to heap retribution on her former friend's sneaky, interfering, devious head at the earliest opportunity, she managed a stiff smile and an even stiffer reply. "She's imagining things. You know Tricia's a dyed-in-the-wool romantic."

Apparently deaf to her denial, he spoke through gritted teeth. "You'll marry that guy over my dead body, Maria!"

Anger at his belligerence overcoming her sense of self-preservation, she snapped, "I'll try and arrange the service to include an execution."

A furiously beating pulse was visible beside his temple, while his gaze sliced through her like tempered steel. "Shut up," he demanded fiercely. "Just shut up, Maria!"

An outraged gasp was lost in movement as her arm was grabbed and she was pulled toward the restaurant's back exit. Swallowing past the knot of panic forming in her throat, she stammered, "Just w-where do you think you're taking me?"

"Where we can talk with some semblance of privacy."

Maria began dragging her feet as well as she could in a pair of three-inch heels, nervously wondering where he was planning to have their little chat. Outside? In his car? Or...? Just let him try taking her

home with him, she thought angrily. Just let him dare!
Slanting him a glance from the corner of her eye, her
heart sank to the level of her tight shoes when she noticed the expression on his face. The way he looked
right now he would dare anything!

His teeth were clenched, his mouth set in a resolute
line, and his square chin was tilted at a stubborn angle. But she had her fair share of obstinance, she decided bracingly, and she wasn't about to let him get
away with this Neanderthal behavior. "Let go of me
this instant," she demanded heatedly. "I don't appreciate being pulled about like a leashed donkey, Mr.
Sinclair."

"Then quit acting like one!"

She had every intention of verbally annihilating him
for the insult, but thought better of it when he
slammed into the free-swinging back door with the
palm of his hand. Her heart instantly leaped into her
throat, and her strained features betrayed the alarm
she felt at the banked fury dictating his actions. As the
heavy door swung open, she wondered what miracle
had kept the rounded, stained-glass panel inset from
shattering into a thousand pieces. She wished it had,
she decided with sudden acrimony. It would serve him
right if he was carted off to jail for malicious damage
to private property.

Avoiding the startled eyes of a couple retrieving
their coats from a smirking cloakroom attendant, she
leaped past Drew with embarrassed haste. Taken by
surprise, he released his hold on her and she stomped
onto the pillared rear veranda in a towering rage of her
own. Sheer momentum propelled her down a wide
graveled footpath that meandered through a formally
arranged garden.

There was a full moon overhead, and her surroundings were bathed by its radiant glow. But she was too upset to appreciate the beauty around her, or the sweet scent rising from the miniature rose hedges that lined the path. Moonlight and roses were too redolent of romance to suit her sour mood, and she almost welcomed the chill breeze that had replaced the earlier heat of late summer. As she reached a nearby copse of tall elm trees and whipped around to face the man following her, the gooseflesh popping out on her skin had nothing to do with the weather and everything to do with the aggressively scowling male looking down at her.

"Have you lost your mind?" she demanded, her hands curling into fists at her sides.

He stared at her with grim resolution. "I'm getting there."

"Well, you can get there on your own," she said with a defiant toss of her head. "I steer clear of madmen, especially rude ones who cause scenes in public."

"I didn't know you took the time to be so discerning," he said with a sneer. "You replaced Phelps with Holcomb quickly enough."

As though disembodied, Maria watched her hand fly through the air in disbelief. Although she'd often been tempted to slap him, the reality as she stared down at her stinging palm was far from pleasant. She wasn't a violent person, and the emotions this man brought out in her were shocking. "I'm sorry," she whispered in an agony of remorse. "I didn't mean to—"

"Didn't you?" he interrupted, the very quietness of his voice causing her to quiver with dread. "I think you did."

Maria's eyes clouded with misery. "You know that's not true."

Slowly his hand rubbed at the reddened flesh on his cheek, a cynical smile curving his mouth. "Do I?"

His trite attitude wiped away guilt and replaced it with increasingly hostile resentment. "I offered you a sincere apology. Do you expect me to grovel?"

Drew's features stilled, his eyes filled with brooding introspection. "I don't know what I expect from you, and I sure as hell don't know what you want from me."

Recovering her lost dignity, Maria greeted his complaint with a tired, dispirited smile. "Does what I want really matter to you?"

"Yes," he stated bluntly. "As much as I hate to admit it, it damn well does!"

Her features reflected the consternation his admission caused her, and she struggled to subdue the momentary tenderness that arose within her at his words. Never having allowed any other man to get this close to that soft, inner core of emotion she kept hidden from the outside world, she was out of her depth and she knew it. She didn't want to care, to be responsible for anyone but herself.

The coolness of her voice reflected this inner determination. "Then I'd like to go back inside now, Drew."

"Are you going to introduce me to your boyfriend, Maria?" Her lashes flickered with nervousness, and he smiled mockingly. "Assuming he's here tonight, of course."

Disconcerted by the sudden shift in topic, she barely managed to keep her face expressionless. "No, he's not."

"That's not very gallant of him," he drawled. "He should be with you, if only to provide you with an escort."

She shifted self-consciously and lowered her eyes before he could see the guilt that assailed her at his words. "Not necessarily," she hedged. "Charlie and I aren't attached at the hip, or anything like that. He has his interests and I have mine."

His lips twisted cynically, his expression darkly introspective as he studied her. "It's odd how my sister's opinion seems to differ from yours. Are you certain you're not hiding your engagement from me, Gypsy?"

She shook her head, her eyes huge dark pools of apprehension. "I told you, any engagement is all in Tricia's imagination. I like being independent."

"If you're so damned independent," he retorted harshly, "then why did you take up with Holcomb in the first place?"

"I think that's my concern."

"No, I really think it's mine," he stated in a voice heavy with accusation. "What's between us goes too deep, doesn't it, Maria? That's why you jumped into an affair with another man so soon after Phelps's death, when you knew damn good and well that I wanted you."

Her mouth formed a disdainful curve. "Maybe I didn't want you, did you ever think of that?"

"Oh, you want me all right," he drawled softly. "You always have, but you chose to become involved with someone who wouldn't pose any threat to your freedom. You don't really give a hoot for this guy."

"I do so," she denied heatedly.

"You're not in control when you're with me," he continued with ruthless persistence, "and you knew I'd never stand back and let you take the upper hand in our relationship. That's why you threw Holcomb at my head in the first place."

His accusation was too close to the truth for comfort, and she decided on sarcasm as her only means of defense. "Goodness, I'm a calculating bitch, and aren't you lucky to have been saved from my clutches? The way you build a case, I'm surprised you're not a prosecuting attorney, Mr. Sinclair. But don't worry, you needn't have anything more to do with me."

"You know I didn't mean—"

Maria sliced the air with her hand, effectively halting his explanation. "Your meaning was crystal clear, but let me set you straight on a couple of minor points, Counselor. First, I have never deliberately used anyone, either male or female. Second, I'm not a taker who gives nothing in return. I assure you that both Charlie and I are perfectly satisfied with our relationship!"

Startled by the fierceness of her response, Drew eyed the mottled flush of rage coloring her cheeks. "You're twisting around everything I say to suit yourself."

Drawing a calming breath into his lungs, he sighed heavily and shook his head. "This isn't getting us anywhere."

An assenting grimace greeted his statement. "You have that right!"

"Get down off your ivory tower, honey," he remarked tiredly. "In case you haven't noticed, this is the real world and men and women have been using each other since time began.''

''Maybe in your world, Drew,'' she murmured firmly, ''but never in mine!''

Although her manner was rife with belligerence, there was a wealth of sadness in the eyes that studied him so intently.

Although he blew an exasperated breath from between pursed lips, there was a thread of amusement in his voice as he asked, ''Why do you suppose we fight every time we share the same space?''

''Don't try changing the subject.'' When his mobile brows quirked with conjecture, Maria knew if she didn't answer his question he'd keep badgering her until she did. ''We fight because we can't stand each other, of course.''

The negative shake of his head was swift and irritatingly confident. ''We fight because we're frustrated,'' he explained gently, ''and frustration often finds a release in aggression.''

Maria realized how right he was, at least on her part, but the knowledge made her more determined than ever to deny his allegations. ''Speak for yourself, mister. I am not the least bit frustrated.''

''Yes you are,'' he argued with newly restored cheerfulness. ''You're also as curious about me as I am about you. Unsatisfied curiosity is also damned frustrating.''

Her mouth slanted with petulance. ''I'm not curious, either.''

He noted the mutinous angle of her chin. ''Are you trying to convince me that you've never once wondered how we would be in bed together?''

His mockery set her teeth on edge, and she struggled to maintain her rapidly disappearing self-control. "My thoughts are not your concern."

"How about your fantasies?" he drawled with maddening persistence.

"Will you stop questioning me?" Maria gave him a look of extreme disfavor, her nails leaving tiny oval crescents in the palms of her hands. "Might I remind you that this is not a courtroom, and I'm not on trial, Counselor?"

His glance encompassed her from head to toe, his eyes wandering over her tense figure with every evidence of pleasure. "Too bad it's not a bedroom."

She inhaled swiftly and a protesting groan escaped from between her parted lips. "Stop this nonsense and let me go back inside."

Expecting another chiding remark, she was surprised when Drew remained silent. Unable to bring herself to look at him, she nervously shifted her weight from one foot to the other. When a group of people left the restaurant and began walking in their direction, she was grateful for the diversion they provided. They were laughing at something one of the women had said as they strolled along the footpath, and Maria suddenly envied them their lightheartedness.

The minor headache she'd suffered earlier in the evening was returning with a vengeance, and she was bone tired and more than a trifle depressed. Arguing with Drew always exhausted her, but more so tonight than usual, thanks to Tricia's machinations. The turncoat had certainly kept her promise not to spill the beans about Maria's true relationship with Charlie, instead doing just the opposite. The wretch had known she'd be inciting Drew to snap at her heels.

The small wave of humanity turned before reaching the shadow-dappled copse where she and Drew were standing, and continued along an alternate path that ended close to the main parking area. Their voices faded as they rounded the corner of the restaurant, and the silence between her and the tense man at her side became charged with too many things left unsaid.

As though in response to their emotional turmoil, there was a sudden shift in the weather. The wind increased in velocity as they stood locked in their own thoughts, and a hint of fog chilled her flesh as she listened to the rustling trees overhead. Wrapping her arms over the thin bodice of her dress, she shivered as the cold penetrated her self-absorption.

Drew noticed the betraying gesture and quickly removed his tuxedo jacket. With a grimace, he placed it around her smooth bare shoulders and said, "I know you won't believe this, but I didn't bring you out here to freeze you to death."

Although it was difficult to maintain her equilibrium with the scent of him in her nostrils and the warmth from his jacket penetrating her body, she responded to the teasing note in his voice with relief. "I'm sure you didn't. A frozen corpse would hardly enhance your sterling reputation in the courtroom."

A slight smile curved his mouth, and she offered no resistance when he linked his fingers through hers and began to move in the direction the other diners had just traversed. As their feet crunched against the graveled path, Maria felt some of her tension disperse. Thus she was taken completely off guard when Drew's quietly insistent voice disrupted the companionable silence that had fallen between them. "Although my questions obviously irritate you, there's one more I need to ask, Maria.''

Lulled by the casualness of his comment, she smiled up at him. ''What is it?''

In unspoken accord they bypassed the rear entrance and continued walking until they had circled the northern edge of the two-story white and rust-trimmed building. They ended up in front of the main entrance, but instead of climbing the wide red brick steps that led to a pair of massive, heavily carved doors, he urged her into the shadows. They stopped beneath the veranda's ivy-shrouded overhang, and the look on Drew's face caused the breath to become trapped in her lungs.

Lights set at either side of the double-doored entry gave out a faint radiance, although the smooth cream-colored globes were too far away to provide any real illumination. But the moon overhead aided her in viewing his face, and the uncharacteristic solemnity of his features caused a ripple of unease to course down her spine. When he spoke, it took her a moment to make sense of his words, but all too soon her mind cleared. At least she thought it did. ''What did you say?'' she asked incredulously.

Drew was annoyed, viewing her hesitancy as a ploy to make this as difficult for him as she could. His expression immediately hardened into one of grim purposefulness, his gaze intense as he sought to interpret her reaction to his question. ''You heard me.''

Certain now that her thoughts were still in a jumble, she shook her head. Her voice a thready whimper that embarrassed her, she asked, ''You want me to...to...?''

''Marry me,'' he said.

Three

Oh, Drew! Please . . . don't do this to me, she wanted to cry out. Don't weave reality into the dreams I've never let myself believe in. Her lashes lowered over eyes suddenly burning with a need to weep, and she bowed her head in defeat. She had to remember why a marriage between them was out of the question if she hoped to prevent the darkness of her past from shadowing Drew's future.

She trembled as she was catapulted back in time, to nightmare surroundings that represented her own private hell. It was a place where the glare of flashing lights pierced the night, where cold bit into unprotected flesh like icy swords, where voices beguiled and beseeched in obscene whispers, and where hunger became a ravening beast demanding satisfaction at any price. . . .

"Aren't you going to answer me, Maria?"

The harshly spoken question made her jump, and her head jerked up to meet his steely eyed gaze. Her mouth opened and closed, then opened again to allow her to drag air into her lungs. Still in shock over his proposal, she said the first thing that came into her head. "What about... what about Charlie?"

A murderous light entered his eyes as he bit out forcefully, "Get rid of him!"

"This is your idea of a joke... right?"

"I only wish it was," he muttered.

Feeling as though her sanity were hanging by a thread, she struggled to get a grip on herself. "You don't sound like an eager bridegroom, so why the proposal?"

"You haven't left me any alternative, Maria."

"I haven't...?" She raked her teeth over her bottom lip, confusion evident in her eyes. "I don't understand."

"Oh, come on!" he retorted impatiently. "I've wanted you for years, and you've finally managed to back me into a corner. I'm not going to stand by and watch you marry another man just to spite me!"

"I'm not marrying Charlie, although I can't see why the possibility should concern you." Her eyes darkened with pain as she remembered how casually he'd reacted when she'd first laid that particular red herring across his path. "My relationship with him didn't seem to bother you before."

"Not bother me?" he demanded through gritted teeth. He flung out his arm in a slashing arc, his eyes shooting sparks as he glared at her. "I've never spent a more miserable Christmas in my life. I listened to you sing that guy's praises until I was tempted to smash everything in sight. For years you'd repelled every overture I'd made to you because of your attachment to Thomas Phelps. After he died I decided to give you a few months to get over the shock, and you became involved with someone else. God, I don't know how I stopped myself from strangling you!"

Stunned by his confession, she murmured faintly, "You were jealous."

He nodded curtly, forcing a smile from his lips. "And judging by my recent behavior, nothing's changed. Poetic justice, isn't it? I was certain that I could come back home and ignore your existence, but one glance and I knew I'd do everything in my power to get you away from that jerk."

"Charlie's not a jerk."

Ignoring her protest, he reached out and enfolded her hands between his warm palms. "While we're together you'll be able to enjoy anything money can buy, and I'll sign a prenuptial agreement entitling you to a generous cash settlement in the event of a divorce."

And one that would no doubt protect his interests as well as her own. At the thought, anguish sliced through her with the viciousness of a tempered blade. He was offering to marry her, but in actuality she'd have no more security than a mistress. In the interim she would enjoy the things his wealth could provide, but she knew she'd never be satisfied with such an emotionless bargain.

Her reluctance to become involved with him had always been motivated by the fear that he would take over her entire being, leaving nothing of herself intact once his passion for her was slaked. She wouldn't be able to prevent herself from demanding more than he was willing to give, and he wouldn't be able to stop himself from growing tired of her. There had been enough goodbyes in her life, she thought with a shiver of revulsion, and she just wasn't willing to risk another.

Some of that fear spilled over into her voice as she replied to his question with the timidity of a woman torn between logic and desire. As much as she wanted to give in to him, she could never marry Drew. She would only end up a liability and could even destroy his career if the news media ever got ahold of the truth about her past. Drew listened to the three words she finally managed to utter, disbelief stamped across his features. "What did you say?" he asked incredulously.

"I said, no thank you."

Her lashes dipped briefly and then rose to reveal the sudden glitter of tears in her eyes. Cursing herself for lowering her defenses so completely, she raised her chin pugnaciously and firmly freed her hands. "I'm sorry, but marriage doesn't figure in my plans for the future."

"What kind of game are you playing, Maria?" He gnashed his teeth together and a muscle pulsed out of control in his jaw. "You knew damn good and well that just the threat of you marrying Holcomb was enough to force my hand."

"No matter what you choose to believe," she stated proudly, "I had nothing to do with making you think I intended to marry Charlie Holcomb. I'll admit that in the beginning I used his presence in my life to discourage you, but it was a spur-of-the-moment decision I've often regretted. While he lived with me we shared a very special relationship, and it was one that should never have been sullied by deception."

His brows quirked devilishly, and his voice held triumph as he asked, "Did you kick him out, or did he leave of his own accord, Maria?"

"I never..." God, he's sharp! Maria thought. He had picked up on her use of the past tense with Machiavellian cleverness and set her up before she'd even begun to suspect that she'd given away the fact that Charlie no longer lived with her. Resisting the urge to stamp her foot like a frustrated child, she muttered, "Mind your own business!"

This time the tender glow in his eyes nearly stopped her heart, and she couldn't make herself look away. She was trapped within that silver stream of sensuousness, her insides melting in response to the message she was receiving from him. "I fully intend to make you my business," he informed her gruffly. "Let me drop Delia off at home and meet you later at your place, and we'll discuss ways and means, Gypsy."

He clasped the soft flesh above her elbows with firm gentleness and began pulling her toward him. The indulgent curve of his mouth mesmerized her, and she felt her feet moving in his direction with numbed acceptance. "That's right," he murmured encouragingly. "Let me show you how good it could be between us. Just give me one night, and I promise you won't suffer any regrets in the morning."

Regrets? The word echoed over and over again in her head, and she struggled to clear her thoughts. "Don't say no," he groaned. "We've already wasted too much time, sweet thing."

Blinking rapidly, she tried to summon up enough willpower to withstand temptation and finally settled on indignation as a way to harden her resolve. She supposed she should be flattered by his persistence, but his easy dismissal of his date for the evening struck a sour note. To her his suggestion seemed to reinforce what she'd always believed about his attitude toward women, that they were amusing diversions but basically unworthy of serious consideration.

The smoldering embers of her temper igniting with satisfying force, she snapped, "You'll do no such thing, Andrew Sinclair. I refuse to be a party to such cavalier treatment of another woman."

Drew's hands momentarily tightened around her wrists, but his narrow-lidded inspection of her features only increased his frustration. "For heaven's sake, woman, I'm not planning to tell Delia my plans for later tonight!"

The mulish obstinacy in her face was worth a thousand words, he thought, and he knew better than to expect her to climb down off her newest soapbox without another fight. His breath exited his lips in a rush, as he released his hold on her and placed a safe distance between them before he gave in to the impulse to force the issue.

Leaning his back against the ivy-cushioned boards of the lower veranda, he shoved his hands into the pockets of his slacks and gave her a conciliatory smile. "Delia has no claim on me," he informed her gently. "We shared a relationship of sorts before I moved to Washington, but this is the first time I've taken her out since I came home."

The quick surge of triumph she felt at his confession was obliterated by the wave of panic that began to well up inside of her. Just the thought of being alone with him in the intimacy of her apartment made her hair stand on end, and she stammered, "I-It will be terribly late by the time y-you drop Delia off, Drew. Another time would be b-better."

"It has to be tonight." With the tenaciousness of a man accustomed to success, he said, "I have to catch a plane for Washington tomorrow afternoon to tie up a few loose ends, and I'll be away for several days. I want things settled between us, Maria."

"I...I have a headache."

There was a brief pause before soft, raspy ripples of laughter greeted the oldest excuse in the history of female Homo sapiens. It was everything she could do not to cringe, especially when he whispered, "Honey, look at me."

Every ounce of sense she possessed warned her to ignore him, but she found herself powerless to resist his quietly spoken appeal. She began to scan his boldly carved features, but the heated look in his eyes caused her to quickly shift her gaze upward. She caught her breath as a sliver of light turned his hair to palest gold, providing a vivid contrast to the dark green leaves at his back.

She vividly remembered what that moon-kissed mane felt like beneath her hands. With compulsive curiosity her gaze shifted to the center of his chest, and she began to visualize the tanned flesh and light dusting of body hair hidden by his white dress shirt. She'd never touched him there, and she wondered if that curly mat would be coarse or soft against her searching fingertips. Would his small brown nipples peak and harden if she kissed them? Her mouth went dry at the thought, and she surreptitiously moistened her lips with the tip of her tongue.

The involuntary action resulted in a brief, succinct expletive being uttered by the man watching her so avidly, and she jumped with a startled gasp. Her head rolled back as though propelled by a powerful magnet, and her heart shifted into overload as she once again inspected Drew's tautening features. He was staring at her mouth, and the unmistakable flicker of desire she saw in the depths of his eyes was both a revelation and a promise.

It was as if he had opened his mind and drawn her inside until she was able to sense the pleasure he'd felt when she looked at him. If she'd had any doubts about the extent of his emotional response to her searching inspection, they were immediately dispelled by the languid parting of lips hungry for the taste of her own.

Blood rushed to Drew's head as Maria continued to stare at him, and he felt almost dizzy with longing. Moonbeams caressed her taut little figure the way he ached to do, and he knew he was dangerously vulnerable to her in that instant. But as he gazed into her haunting black eyes and felt a burning need for satisfaction in his throbbing loins, putting out the fire was all that mattered. Without pausing to think, his hands spanned her narrow waist and he drew her forward until there was no longer any distance between them.

Her pitifully weak effort at resistance was greeted by a devastatingly masculine grin, and her pulse leaped in response. His darkening gaze held sensual secrets that caused every inch of her body to prickle with an awareness she was powerless to deny, and an enervating weakness attacked her muscles. It was a mind-blowing sensation she'd never experienced with any other man and one that was seductively addictive.

Maria's breathing became labored, while her most secret flesh softened and grew moist with shocking suddenness. Although lacking in practical experience, she wasn't so innocent that she didn't realize the full significance of her body's betrayal. When bold hands cupped her buttocks and urged her against a hotly aroused masculine frame, what little resistance she had left disappeared beneath an overpowering surge of desire.

His jacket slid from her shoulders to the ground, but she didn't mourn the loss of its warmth. Her body was generating its own heat, with the help of a mouth intent on devouring every inch of her exposed flesh. A tiny moan slipped from her throat as his eager lips spread a trail of fire across her shoulders, and she fought to replenish the oxygen in her lungs as she mindlessly clutched at his strong neck.

"Yes," he growled, his tongue tasting the frantic pulse that beat against the vulnerable hollow of her throat. "Hold me tight and feel what you're doing to me, sweet thing."

She began to comply, her thoughts whirling into the stratosphere. But before her hands could begin to make their own demands, one of the heavy doors above them swung open. The noise and garish light that emerged from the interior of the restaurant successfully dispelled their illusion of privacy, causing them to jerk apart as they were brutally brought back to an awareness of their surroundings.

For long, silent moments their heated glances sought to retain the former closeness of their bodies, until a disgruntled voice cried, "Maria, I've been looking for you everywhere. It's time for you to..."

Tricia's voice trailed off uncertainly as she stepped onto the veranda and spotted her brother. "Why, Drew," she said with a self-conscious laugh. "I didn't realize you were out here. I mean, I thought Maria was still hiding . . . um, busy in the ladies' room, and Delia said you'd gone out for some fresh air. But of course I never—''

Drew interrupted his sister's stammering explanation with a stilted laugh that failed to sound in the least amused. ''Don't trip over your tongue, brat. You achieved your purpose, so go back inside. Maria and I will follow you in a minute.''

''You'd better make it quick,'' she retorted with a delighted grin. ''Delia's been frothing at the mouth for the last half hour.''

Mention of the other woman broke the spell that had held Maria in thrall. With a muttered excuse she bent to pick up Drew's jacket and practically threw it at him in her haste to escape. Avoiding the hand that reached out to stop her, she circled the seductive devil who was temptation personified and ran up the steps. She caught a glimpse of the excited speculation in Tricia's eyes but scurried past her like a frightened rabbit.

She was definitely not in the mood to satisfy her friend's curiosity, especially when said friend's overactive tongue had helped to get her into this mess in the first place. Indeed, Maria doubted if she could answer her own questions at the moment. Thoughts were whirling dervishes in her brain, her confusion so great she had to pause in the entry foyer to recoup both her breath and her sense of direction.

Immediately her neck prickled with awareness, and a soft expulsion of breath wafted against her ear as strong fingers clasped her upper arms and pulled her back against a hard body. ''A temporary reprieve, Gypsy,'' came the whispered warning.

About to utter a caustic remark, her plans were foiled with frustrating quickness. A deep, grating laugh erupted from Drew's chest, and she was released with a suddenness that caused her to stumble. He walked past her as though nothing untoward had happened, one finger looped around the collar of the slightly crumpled jacket flung over his shoulder.

Although he moved with languid grace, his long legs traversed the crowded room much too quickly to suit her. He spoke briefly to Delia before seating himself, but obviously the other woman wasn't satisfied with a verbal explanation. She scooted closer to his side and wrapped her arms around his neck, her lush mouth parting in unspoken demand. Maria hurriedly averted her eyes, but the evasive action wasn't quick enough to prevent her from seeing their lips meet.

This just proves how right I was to refuse to take him seriously, she decided angrily. If he can propose to me one minute and let that redheaded harpy maul him the next, he wasn't the prize husband material he thought himself to be. And even if he is, a caustic inner voice reminded, you can't take him up on his offer.

The truth was so painful she wanted to cry out at the unfairness of life, but the only sound that emerged from her mouth was a muffled gasp. She couldn't change the past or wipe away what she'd done so long ago, she thought sadly, and railing against fate was a useless enterprise guaranteed to drive her insane.

A curiously subdued Tricia joined her, but Maria was completely deaf to her guilty attempts to strike up a conversation. As they walked toward their table, she was preoccupied with raising new defenses against Drew. I don't care who he kisses, she told herself, repeating the thought several times in a frantic attempt to bring some sort of order to her mind. *Dear God, please don't let me care!*

Maria sat with her chin propped in her hand and pensively gazed into space. One elbow rested upon the walnut-grained surface of her desk while her other hand was busy rolling a pencil between her fingers. During this past, interminable week, she hadn't been able to get her mind off a certain sexy blond man with broad shoulders and banked fires in his eyes, and the failure was making her a nervous wreck.

The sudden shrill peal of the phone in front of her caused her to jerk clumsily, and her pencil went sailing halfway across the beige-carpeted floor. Muttering an imprecation beneath her breath while alternately praying her caller wasn't Drew, she groped for the telephone receiver with a hand that shook visibly. "Hello, Maria Fairmont speaking."

"Maria, you've got to help me," a harassed male demanded. "If you don't I might get desperate."

She recognized Charlie's voice instantly. A pleased smile spread itself across her face, and there was a marked undercurrent of affection in her questioning response. "What desperate act are you contemplating, Mr. Holcomb?"

"I'll send my baby sister over to make your life miserable."

Since blond, blue-eyed Lynette was the apple of both of their eyes, his threat was an empty one. "Try again, handsome."

A husky laugh greeted her retort. "Then *I'll* move back in with you and make your life miserable."

Maria greeted this newest warning with a derisive gurgle of laughter, remembering how hard she'd tried to convince Charlie to remain with her after he graduated from high school. She had wanted to help him through college the way Tom had helped her, but had understood his need to prove himself capable of providing an adequate home for his sister on his own.

This past couple of months, she'd rattled around in her apartment like a lost soul. Although their new home was only a short elevator ride away, it wasn't the same as having them live with her. But Charlie was coping well with his new responsibilities, and her voice reflected her pride in him. "That's no penance, Charlie. It's deadly dull without you around here to tease me, and I even miss Lynette adding mayhem to my mornings. My makeup case is being sadly neglected."

"Well, the one you bought her for her birthday certainly isn't. Right now she and her friends have bottles and tubes spread all over the bathroom counter. You shouldn't have spent so much money on her, Maria."

She uttered a small, distinctive grunt. "That's rich, coming from the brother who just forked out a bundle on a top-of-the-line ten-speed."

Charlie immediately expressed anxiety. "Do you think she's getting spoiled?"

"Don't be a nit brain, Charlie."

Maria's indignant response caused him to choke on an indrawn breath, and his voice was still a trifle raspy when he asked, "Is that any way for a lady to talk?"

"It is when a gentleman asks stupid questions."

"Ever Lynette's champion, aren't you, angel?"

"With just cause." A sudden image of Drew rose up in her mind, adding a caustic note to her voice. "We women have to stick together, or you men would ride roughshod all over us. And to correct your mistaken assumption, Lynette's the angel, not me."

"That's what you think!"

His disgruntled response brought another smile to her face. "Uh-oh! What's she been up to now? The last time you were in this mood she'd been bugging you to let her frost her hair."

"What's she been up to?" he repeated dolefully. "I'm nice enough to let her have a sleep-over as well as a skating party at the ice rink for her birthday, and what do I get?"

"What do you get, Charlie?"

"Four teenage females making goo-goo eyes at me and a smirking sister who encourages them, that's what I get! They're already driving me crazy. When did little girls become so aggressive, Maria?"

His question held such an aggrieved note, she barely managed to suppress the giggles bubbling in her throat. "I think it started with big girls. Something called women's lib, Charlie my boy."

"Well, it's enough to turn a guy's hair gray, and as if I don't have enough problems, my shower head just fell off and nearly bashed my skull in."

Her shoulders began to shake as she considered his predicament, and she quickly clapped a hand over her mouth as a preventive measure. Eventually regaining her shattered poise, she said, "I'll call the maintenance man, but in the meantime you can use my shower."

"You're a lifesaver!"

His usual good humor completely restored, he promised, "Be there in the twinkle of an eye, angel."

She laughed at her friend's eagerness. "I'm still finishing up in the office. Just bang on the door and I'll let you in."

Four

Less than five minutes later Maria heard the sound of Charlie's distinctive, light-knuckled rap. With a casual greeting she gestured him inside and turned to reset the lock. Heading across the room toward the door that led into her apartment, Charlie followed so closely he almost ran her down when she paused to flick on the hallway light.

Maneuvering around his muscular frame, she sent him an amused over-the-shoulder glance as she twisted the bolt lock on the door. Giving him a little shove to speed him on his way, she said, "You know where the bathroom is, so get a move on. Oh, and there's an unscented bar of glycerin soap in the dish above the hand basin. I wouldn't want you to leave here smelling like a flower, Charlie. It might destroy your macho image, and I'd hate to disillusion your young admirers."

He paused long enough to blow a raspberry in her direction before proceeding down the hall and disappearing into the bathroom. As the door closed behind him, she chuckled and lifted her arms over her head in a much-needed stretch. Standing on the tips of her toes, she arched her back with languid enjoyment. A yawn caught her by surprise, reminding her that she was in dire need of a caffeine fix to get her through the rest of the evening.

A glitter of anticipation in her eyes, she began to move toward the kitchen with revitalized enthusiasm. After preparing her coffee maker, she decided to use the time while it brewed to slip into something a little more comfortable. Once again negotiating the hallway, she entered her bedroom and closed the door behind her. Barely glancing at the white wicker furniture and pale rose-colored walls, she quickly stripped down to a pair of frilly bikini panties.

Crossing to her closet, she slid open the mirrored door and studied the garments hanging from the rail. She pulled out a pair of well-washed jeans, the denim soft and flexible as she slid them up her legs. Then she automatically reached for one of her favorite blouses, a sleeveless cotton in an attractive shade of apricot.

With the ease of long practice, she pulled the pins from her hair and stood in front of her white and rose trimmed dressing table while she quickly ran a brush through the thick black strands. It flowed past her waist in a straight dark curtain, and for about the millionth time she found herself wishing it had at least a smidgeon of curl. She looked like a gypsy, she decided, scowling with sudden rancor at the thought.

The hated nickname reminded her of Drew at his aggravating best. Not for the first time, she wondered

how such a sweet, good-natured woman like Tricia
had ended up related to him. She'd once suggested that
he might be a changeling, and after Tricia had managed to stop laughing, she'd shot down that theory by
pointing out the physical characteristics she shared
with her brother. Maria had grudgingly conceded her
point, but only after arguing the possibility of an in-
fant Drew having been taken over by an alien intelli-
gence right out of the nursery.

Emphasizing her thoughts with an audible sniff, she
decided it was time to get her tiny little mind back on
track. Thinking about Drew was not only a waste of
time, it was also guaranteed to make her crazy. As
usual she chose to forgo house shoes and stomped out
of her bedroom with bare feet and a lingering gleam
of aggression in her eyes. But as she passed the bathroom door, some of her inner agitation was lessened
when Charlie burst into song.

She grimaced in sympathy with the walls. The ca-
cophony sounded like two tomcats going at it over the
back fence, and she chuckled at the aptness of the
comparison. Her carrot-topped friend might have the
looks of a modern-day Adonis, she decided with a return of good spirits, but she had a sneaking hunch he
had a tin ear.

Maria was halfway across her living room when the
sound of a buzzer stopped her in her tracks. Her
mouth firming with annoyance, she reluctantly headed
toward the gray panel inset into the wall of her entryway. Pausing to inhale the aroma now emanating from
the kitchen, she resigned herself to having to wait for
her coffee and depressed the switch on her intercom.
"Good evening, may I help you?"

"You may," a lazy voice responded. "Let me in, sweet thing."

As she recognized that deep, sensual rasp, the soft down at the base of her neck stood on end. So did her stomach, a thousand butterflies adding to the internal maelstrom. Swallowing past the panic threatening to close her throat, she splayed her fingers against her parted lips. Not now, she thought, her breath coming in frantic, strangulated puffs. No, she wasn't ready for this yet. If Drew would just wait a little while, say until the year 2050, she would be better prepared for this confrontation. By then she'd either be senile or dead, and the way she felt right now the second alternative was preferable.

Even though she'd spent more hours thinking about him than she wanted to admit, she still wasn't ready to deal with him face-to-face. Why hadn't he phoned first, given her some kind of warning? Because he knew you'd run for the hills, an imp of honesty inside of her head replied. She drew back and stared suspiciously at the communication system, and found herself wondering if Drew had begun reading her mind.

Disconcerted by the possibility, she said the first thing that came into her head. "To whom am I speaking?"

The ensuing silence spoke for itself, but she brushed aside the certainty that to continue in this vein was guaranteed to infuriate her unwanted caller. But she was here and he was there, she decided with convoluted accuracy, momentarily emboldened by a false sense of security. Although he walked the earth with the panache of a superman, he still wasn't able to leap tall buildings with a single bound.

Maria might have been calmed by the absurdity of her thoughts if Drew hadn't chosen that instant to roar at her like a wounded lion. "Dammit woman, will you unlock this door? It's hot out here!"

She ached to send him where it was hotter but decided now was certainly not the time to let her irritation get in the way of good judgment. To lose control was to place oneself at a decided disadvantage, which was something she definitely couldn't afford when dealing with him.

The bellow came again, more forcefully than before. "Maria!"

"What?" she screamed, jumping back and clutching at her chest with a shaking hand.

"God, you didn't have to deafen me," he bit out, his complaint uttered in disgusted accents. With a long-suffering air, he coaxed, "Come on, honey. Buzz me inside before I get sunstroke."

Taking a few more seconds to give her erratic heartbeat a chance to shift out of high gear, she glared at the intercom as though it were responsible for her plight. Then she slammed her palm against the button that would release the lock on the lobby entrance and gritted her teeth as she headed for her front door. With a fatalistic sigh she stepped into her entryway and shivered as her feet made contact with the cool ceramic tile.

At least that was the justification she chose in order to account for the goose bumps popping out on her flesh. She could feel the provocative pout of her nipples against the thin material of her blouse and at the same time found herself wishing that her neckline wasn't cut quite so low. Giving her bodice a sharp, upward tug, she also wished the light material didn't cling to her body like a drift of mist.

Throwing her front door open with a confident precision that would have done any drill sergeant proud, she crossed her arms over her chest and stepped out into a green-carpeted hallway. Mere seconds later Drew rounded the corner that led off the central lobby, five feet eleven inches of compact muscle with a scowl ferocious enough to intimidate Satan himself and the loping stride of a stalking beast in search of prey.

As had happened before, she was struck by his similarity to a golden-coated puma...sleek, powerful, dangerous. Studying the sinuous movements of his superbly conditioned body, her mouth went as dry as the Sahara. Barely a week ago she had refused to marry this man, and if she wasn't mistaken he was still a mite sore at her.

He certainly seemed capable of taking a few bites out of someone, she decided nervously, and it wasn't going to be her. Deliberately allowing their eyes to meet, she let him know with a glance that she was on the defensive. Her attitude, unfortunately, didn't seem to intimidate him in the least. Those silver orbs of his held determination, purpose and unmistakable heat as they wandered over her.

"Hi, sweet thing," he murmured. "My business in Washington took longer than I'd planned. Did you miss me?"

Like a toothache, she thought, too cowardly to utter the taunt out loud. Understandably enough, the idea of goading him just to get his juices flowing didn't even occur to her. His juices appeared to be doing fine without any help from her, and the last thing she wanted to do right now was to provoke him into a repeat of last Saturday night. Keep it cool, Maria, she told herself. Keep things cool and uncomplicated.

"I think I'm going to live after all, angel," Charlie said as he appeared in the doorway. "Thanks for letting me use your shower."

Oh, my God . . . she'd forgotten about Charlie! As he stood next to her, she could have sworn she saw fire flash from Drew's eyes. As nervous as a cat on a dog's back, she quickly mumbled an introduction. "Charlie, this is Andrew Sinclair. Drew, meet Charles Holcomb, a . . . um . . . a neighbor of mine."

By this time Drew had done a few calculations in his mind, and he was furious at the conclusions he'd reached. The description Maria had once given him of the great love of her life fit this guy to perfection, but he was just a kid! A wet-behind-the-ears, snotty-nosed kid! What the hell was she doing with a young pup barely old enough to shave? As he took in the muscular physique and handsome face of the young man in question an answer presented itself, but it was one he never for one instant contemplated.

Maria was a naturally seductive little baggage, but the only thing she'd be interested in doing with a boy this age was mothering him. He studied the youth at her side with narrow-eyed conjecture, and it was as though a light flashed on in his brain. So she enjoyed playing games, did she...stupid, infantile games. The minx, the lying, deceitful, sneaky . . . !

For the better part of a year and a half he'd been insanely jealous of a child! It made him wonder how many other diversions she'd thrown in his path over the years, and it took a great deal of effort to prevent himself from voicing the bitter accusations pounding in his brain. Maria had not only made a fool of him, he decided with rapidly escalating ire, but she had compounded the offense by involving his own sister in her schemes.

He opened his mouth to let fly at her, but closed it again with a snap. Why should he betray his new knowledge, when faking ignorance would give him such a delicious edge in getting some of his own back? The devious little witch certainly deserved to be taught a lesson. All he had to do was play her game, merely bending the rules a bit to give him the advantage. He was going to enjoy himself at her expense for a change...damn right he was!

As he planned his revenge, a trace of amusement lightened his darkening mood. It was time Ms. Maria Fairmont received a dose of her own medicine, and he was just the man to hold her pert little nose and make her swallow. With a smile that was a masterpiece of conviviality and a voice that was as smooth as silk, he murmured, "Surely Mr. Holcomb is more than a mere neighbor, Maria. I would think only a very good...friend would be invited to use your shower."

The hand Maria lifted to her throat clenched until she was in danger of strangling herself, and she awkwardly lowered her arm to her side. "Well, yes, no...I mean..."

His eyes lacerated her with the double-edged sword of mockery and contempt even as he tilted his head in inquiry. "Charles," he repeated musingly. Then he slapped the heel of his palm against his forehead and widened his eyes with feigned innocence. "Of course...this is the Charlie you once told me about."

"Yes, well...not exactly. You see, I...he..."

He ignored her garbled response and instead concentrated on her companion's bewildered features.

Reaching out to clasp Charlie's hand, he shook it briefly. "You and Maria lived together at one time, didn't you, Mr. Holcomb?"

Nervously Charlie glanced toward Maria and stiffened with aggressiveness as he noticed the panic-stricken look in the eyes she kept trained on Drew. Following the direction of her gaze, he was instantly intimidated by the sheer poise and self-confidence of the other man. Jerking his hand to his side, he muttered, "What if we did?"

But Drew refrained from a reply, satisfied with the pleading expression on Maria's face when she looked at him. She wouldn't want to embroil her young friend in this situation and was becoming a wee bit uncomfortable. Good, let her stew for a while, he thought with suppressed violence. It would serve her right for all the sleepless nights she'd caused him.

While Drew was in the process of congratulating himself, the ensuing silence made Maria want to scream with frustration. She barely restrained the urge, although she was quickly becoming anxious enough to do anything that might give her an idea of what he was thinking. But he wasn't giving anything away, his face as revealing as a hunk of granite.

Was he angry enough to deliberately cause her embarrassment, she wondered, dismayed at the possibility. She knew she would never lose Charlie's affection, but she also valued his respect. He was hardly more than a boy, and unusually innocent for his age. Surely Drew wouldn't disillusion him just to get even with her? No, even he couldn't be so cruel.

But before she could be reassured by the thought, she sneaked a sideways glance at her young friend. As though seeing him for the first time, she was shocked to notice how snugly his stone-washed jeans fit him. And surely the musculature of his chest was unusually well-defined? Growing more uncomfortable by the second, she realized that although she considered Charlie a kid, albeit a big one, Drew might have gained a very different impression.

Five

Maria muffled a groan and quickly averted her eyes from the still-damp body beside her. Unfortunately the maneuver placed Drew in her peripheral vision, which proved to be a tactical error. He was staring down at the overnight bag that Charlie was clutching in his hand like a potential weapon, and she didn't like the expression on his face. Why didn't he say something? she wondered with increasing discomposure. When was he going to blurt out the truth and let Charlie know how she'd lied through her back teeth about him?

Just then Drew's head rose, and his beautifully sculpted mouth twisted into an ugly, cynical curve as his gaze shifted from her to the boy at her side. She inhaled on a gasp, her earlier suspicion becoming a certainty. Surely he didn't still think that she and Charlie...that they were...? The filthy-minded animal! she thought in shocked incredulity. Glaring at him, tears blurred her vision. Obviously his opinion of her morals was even lower than she'd imagined, and the knowledge left her inwardly writhing beneath this newest blow to her pride.

Determined to prevent her tears from falling down her cheeks, she withstood his cutting glance to the best of her ability. Although her long dark lashes flickered with the need to block him from her sight, she managed to keep her attention centered solely on his condemning face. Other than being caught out in a bold-faced lie, she had nothing to be ashamed of where Charlie was concerned, she consoled herself staunchly, and she was damned if she was going to act as if she did!

Maria tilted her nose so high in the air she knew she'd drown if the fire alarm set off the ceiling sprinklers. Drew's lips began to twitch into a taunting grin, and in resentful fascination she watched as her nemesis crossed both arms over his chest. He knew he'd gotten to her, and he was enjoying every moment of his triumph. The self-righteous jackass, she thought, as a low, raspy chuckle burst from his throat. She gave him a glare filled with warning, but all he did was lean against the wall nearest him with maddening nonchalance. Well, his negligent pose didn't fool her for a moment. His posture was meant to intimidate, but it wasn't going to work with her. She only wished the same could be said for Charlie.

Her friend was looking distinctly uptight, and no wonder. Maria could almost feel the masculine challenge emanating from Drew's taut frame, could see it spewing into life and mingling with the mockery in his eyes as he studied her companion's scowling youthfulness. How dare he look at Charlie with such derision? she thought indignantly. Why shouldn't he? her nagging conscience informed her with merciless honesty. If you hadn't made up all those lies this wouldn't be happening.

But no matter how much she blamed herself, the black-hearted devil had no right to eye her friend as though he were a particularly loathsome bug. It would serve Drew right if she threw her arms around the younger man's neck, just to confirm those vile suspicions slithering around in his brain. And she would do it, too, if she wasn't almost certain that Charlie would laugh and completely spoil the effect.

By now almost ready to explode with resentment, she snapped at her tormentor with increased aggression. "Why don't you go home?"

Drew's smile openly taunted her. "I just got here."

"Well, you can just go away again."

"Not until we finish discussing our future plans, Maria."

"We don't have any plans to discuss."

Widening her eyes with assumed innocence, she perched her hands on her hips and silently dared him to say anything more personal in front of a witness. To her dismay, he took up the challenge. "Does a late summer moon and the scent of roses remind you of anything, honey?" he asked.

A vivid blush colored her cheeks, but her lower lip pushed forward mutinously. "Not a thing."

As he studied the delectable fullness of that pouting mouth, Drew was surprised by the force of the desire that surged through his body. Damn, the things he didn't want to do to this woman! If they were alone he'd press her against the wall and at least slake a portion of his passion with a thrusting tongue, but for now he'd have to contain his impatience.

His chest expanded on a breath, and he murmured, "Don't worry, Maria. After your...friend leaves, it'll be my pleasure to refresh your memory." Making no attempt to disguise the hungry intensity of his emotions, his voice sounded heavy and languid with suppressed need.

Disturbed by the sensuality rife in the other man's suggestive demeanor, Charlie immediately bristled. "Go take a hike, buddy," he muttered, glowering fiercely. "I'm not leaving Maria alone here with you."

She stiffened, her mouth rounding in disbelief. "Oh, glory!"

Her muttered exclamation drew two pairs of eyes in her direction, and Drew felt like laughing out loud. She fully expected him to lose his temper and tear a strip off the boy, and was terrified of what he might say. Good! For a change he was the one with the edge, and he planned to keep it that way. Let the fibbing little wretch suffer for her sins. He'd just have to see how much more he could make her squirm before she discovered he was on to her!

With clipped sarcasm he referred to her erstwhile advocate, his low tones cruelly ridiculing. "So this is your knight in shining armor, honey. A little young for the job, isn't he?"

Stoking the fire of Charlie's resentment, he added, "You certainly believe in extremes. First you latch on to an old geezer you could run circles around, and now you've snared a grass-green adolescent who needs his hand held crossing a street. I wonder what you'll do with a man you can meet on equal ground, Gypsy."

In that instant Charlie drew back his arm, the poised rigidity of his body making his intention plain. Too flustered to retaliate verbally with any degree of credibility, Maria clutched at him before he could do more than clench his fist. "Now...there's no need to get upset, love. This is Mr. Sinclair's way of having a good time. He has a perverted sense of humor, and can't help acting like an idiot on occasion.

"And that's one of the nicer names Lynette is going to call you if you're late," she babbled on anxiously. "By now she's probably a basket case, so you'd better get home before she shows up here complete with her entourage."

"Lynette?" Drew drawled inquiringly. "I didn't realize you had a wife waiting at home, Mr. Holcomb."

"Lynette's my sister," Charlie informed him with a snarl. "Wanna make something of it?"

So he'd been right about Maria's mothering instincts, Drew thought in satisfaction, only there had been two fledglings in her nest. Feeling suddenly exultant, he responded to the boy's bluster with commendable calm. "I wouldn't dream of it, son. You just run along now and get home to your sister."

As though deaf in one ear and unable to hear out of the other, Charlie grabbed Maria and yanked her against his side. He inclined his head in the direction of the lobby without once taking his eyes off the older man. "After you, mister."

Maria watched the shock register on Drew's mobile features, and inwardly cringed. It was apparent that Charlie's insolence was getting to him, and she knew she was going to end up a blithering idiot if she didn't get a certain young man away from here. Of all the times Charlie could have picked for his protective instincts to run rampant, she decided on the edge of panic, this had to be the worst.

A febrile glitter flashed in Drew's eyes. "You want to make a bet on who leaves first, kid?"

Now desperate to defuse the situation before Charlie really put Drew's nose out of joint, Maria racked her brain for a diversion. Unfortunately, her champion chose to retaliate before she could think of a solution.

"Are you going to take me on, old man?" he sneered.

Old man? "Oh, help!" she muttered.

Closing her eyes, she wondered what she'd ever done to deserve this. After a few moments her lashes lifted with unwilling sluggishness, and her gaze collided with that of her tormentor. "Do you want your pretty boy to live long enough to collect his social security?" Drew questioned softly.

The warning made every hair follicle on her body stand up and take notice, but didn't seem to do the same for Charlie. In fact, the remark only seemed to prod him into further stupidity, and his fingers tightened around her shoulder with bone-crushing force. He eyed his unexpected adversary with all the foolish optimism of the very young, his truculent voice filled with forced bravado. "Maria's coming with me!"

Gently Drew murmured, "Maria?"

For an instant her mind went blank, but then a way out presented itself in a flash of what she liked to think of as divine inspiration. From somewhere she dredged up a passable peal of laughter and cocked her head toward Charlie as she willed her mouth to form an amused grimace. She thought her face was going to crack with the effort, but she managed to look convincing. At least she hoped she did. If not she supposed she could try a swoon...it always worked in the Regency romances she enjoyed reading.

When she opened her mouth she discovered herself to be alarmingly short of breath. Praying her voice would hold out long enough to tease Charlie into a better frame of mind, she wheezed, "Thanks for the invitation, but I think I'll pass, love. Ice-skating is not my forte, and I'd be risking life and limb if I accompanied you tonight." In more ways than one, she tacked on mentally.

Charlie lowered his head to mutter a protest in her ear. "I'm not leaving you alone with this character, Maria. I don't like his looks."

She glanced across at the superb form stuffed into well-fitting gray slacks and a maroon dress shirt perfectly contoured to his body, and wondered how anyone could complain about Drew's looks. Pushing the inconsequential thought aside, she whispered, "Don't worry, he's harmless."

She mentally begged God not to strike her dead for that particular lie and gave Charlie's arm a reassuring squeeze. Leaning against his muscle-bound frame for balance, she retained the use of his ear to prevent them from being overheard. "He's Tricia's brother, sweetie. No one for you to worry about."

"What?"

Charlie's yelp was accompanied by a backward jerk of his upper torso, a movement that almost landed Maria on her backside. "You mean this...this big ape is the guy Tricia swears is a direct descendant of Saint Michael's?"

Her laughter echoed down the hallway. As she sneaked a peek at Drew, the compressed line of his lips betrayed his displeasure at being excluded from their conversation. Not at all dismayed by the rudeness of her behavior, she burrowed even closer against the comforting solidity of Charlie's side. "When he's in a temper, I think he looks more like Godzilla than King Kong."

It took Maria a couple of minutes to stop giggling, but eventually she asked, "Don't you think so, Charlie?"

The attempt at levity didn't seem to aid in reassuring her stalwart friend, whose doubtful expression hadn't altered by one iota. "Are you sure you don't want me to hang around and run interference?" he whispered uneasily.

"Of course not," she lied with true valor, not certain at all. "Drew and I have always rubbed each other the wrong way, but I can handle him."

As if to prove her wrong, the man in question stepped forward with visible impatience. "If you are through whispering together like a couple of school kids, I'd like to get a move on, Maria. I have a busy evening scheduled."

And to hell with what you might have planned, Maria, she tacked on silently, rebelling at his high-handedness. But she resisted the urge to stick her tongue out at him and merely said, "Why certainly, Mr. Sinclair."

Turning to Charlie, she gave her pseudo brother an affectionate kiss on his cheek. "Have a good time tonight, and give Lynette my love."

Hugging Maria tightly, he nodded. "We won't be leaving for another half hour, so call me if you change your mind and decide to come along. By then you'll probably be ready for a little light relief, angel.''

Charlie started to walk away but paused suddenly in front of Drew. His manner was touchingly sincere as he warned, ''If you hurt her in any way, you'll answer to me!''

Drew stared at his departing back and muttered, ''Cocky little hothead, isn't he?''

''He reminds me of someone else I know, only you aren't little.''

His mouth twisted wryly. ''Neither is he.''

The admission held a humorous inflection but still managed to rekindle her earlier suspicion. Although she tried to disguise the pain that suspicion had caused her, her voice quivered betrayingly. ''Charlie's like a brother to me, you nasty, evil-minded, stupid—''

''I never doubted it for a moment,'' he interrupted smoothly.

''—obnoxious . . . you what?''

Maria's incredulous howl was accompanied by movement. Forgetting her shoeless state, she lifted her foot and kicked him just above his leather-shod foot. He merely grunted, while for her the pain that shot up her leg was the last straw. ''I hope you enjoyed making me look like a seducer of innocents,'' she yelled through a haze of tears.

Drew's eyes glinted with renewed anger. ''Just like you enjoyed lying to me about your relationship with Charlie Holcomb, Maria? Hell, you even used my own sister to continue the deception.''

Flushing guiltily, she muttered, ''You were trying to seduce me!''

''And you wanted me badly enough to be afraid I'd succeed,'' he countered swiftly.

Embarrassed by the intimacy of their conversation, Maria glanced self-consciously at the other doors leading off the hallway. "You'd better come inside."

The invitation was grudging at best, but there was a satisfied smile on Drew's face as he watched her whirl around abruptly and stomp across her living room with her nose in the air. She reached the sliding glass doors on the other side of the room and stared out at the star-studded night sky.

Quietly Drew closed the door and followed her. "How was it that the Holcomb kids came to live with you?"

When she realized how close he was, she started to step aside, but he reached out and clasped her shoulders between his strong hands. Although her back stiffened defensively at his touch, she stopped trying to evade him. With a sigh she responded to his question, her low tones holding a wealth of sadness. "The authorities were going to separate them, so Charlie took his little sister and ran. I found them hiding in one of my empty units."

"They were orphaned?"

"Their father ran out on them when Lynette was little more than a toddler, and from what I've gathered, Verna Holcomb wasn't exactly the maternal type. It seems she was rarely at home, preferring the company of a succession of men than that of her children. She finally found one who was willing to marry her, but from what Charlie overheard he and Lynette weren't part of the deal. One afternoon she left with her boyfriend, and she never came back."

"Charming," he said with a wince of compassion.

As though her forthrightness brought Drew to his senses, he became aware of how tightly his fingers

were digging into her arms. Quickly easing his grip, he
noticed the faint reddening of her tender skin. Shame
at his unintentional brutality coursed through him,
and he began to smooth away the marks with the pads
of his thumbs. "Why didn't you place them in one of
your shelters?"

Maria tried to ignore the leap of her senses at his
touch and hurriedly resumed speaking. "Charlie was
only sixteen and still in high school, and FACES
doesn't have the proper facilities to deal with mi-
nors."

"Wasn't there anywhere else they could have
gone?"

She glanced at him over her shoulder, a disconcerted frown forming between her brows as she mentioned a mutual friend. "Donovan Lancaster would
have taken them in, but his shelter for runaways isn't
able to provide much more than a couple of hot meals
and a pallet on the floor. He wouldn't have questioned them too closely, but he couldn't have pre-
vented the authorities from searching his premises.
Charlie would have figured that out for himself, and
run away again."

Her voice faded until it was a mere whisper of
sound, and Drew felt the shudder that rippled through
her body. "I just couldn't stand the thought of them
ending up on the streets."

Suddenly Maria twisted against Drew's hands and
leaned against the sliding glass door. She could no
longer bear his touch, but she kept her expression
carefully guarded. The need to retreat had nothing to
do with him and everything to do with the terrible
memories that always left her feeling soiled.

She recalled how, like Charlie, she had once opted for freedom over security. Freedom, she thought with a shiver, sickness coiling in her stomach as she remembered some of the lessons she'd been forced to learn on the streets. But she hadn't been alone in her misery. There had been other kids like her, who had clung to one another because they had no one else.

On a recent news broadcast she'd heard them referred to as "children of the night," which in her opinion was a misnomer. Those frightened, helpless human beings were prisoners of the darkness. They had fallen through the cracks of an impersonal social system that forced them to hide from the light of discovery as they shared what shelter and food they could find.

Maria was so preoccupied with thoughts of the past that, when he spoke, Drew's voice seemed to come to her from a great distance. "Is that what happened to you, Maria? Did Phelps take you off the streets and into his home?"

"Yes," she whispered, her eyes misting as the memories tore at her.

She lowered her lashes, but still she saw faces filled with despair, degradation and hopelessness. Faces old before their time. Faces that still haunted her sleep. Tom had saved her from that shadowed existence, only he'd come into her life too late to prevent the ugliness from touching her. But it hadn't been too late for Charlie and Lynette, and she'd been willing to do anything to prevent them from accumulating the kind of scars that never healed.

Drew was disturbed by the distress on Maria's face. Obviously the thoughts going through her mind were far from pleasant, and he felt a sudden need to ease her tension, to chase away the bitterness from her eyes. It was a protective urge that surprised him, coming as it had on the trailing edge of his anger. "You care a great deal for those kids, don't you?"

"They're the brother and sister I never had."

There was such a wealth of love in her eyes as she glanced into the distance, he found himself wondering how he would feel if that look was for him. He felt his stomach muscles clench as though a blow had landed square in his gut. He didn't want to be this vulnerable with her, he thought, especially when he remembered how adamant she'd been when she'd refused to marry him.

Maria might want him physically, but she sure as hell didn't feel any affection for him. Not the way she had for Tom Phelps, and the thought resurrected all his old resentment and jealousy. "Apparently young Charlie feels the same way about you, if the nickname he's given you is any indication."

When she frowned in momentary confusion, he rasped a single word like an accusation. "Angel!" His lips twisting with mockery, he laughed low in his throat. "Doesn't he know you were once an old man's darling?"

With an outraged gasp, Maria planted her fists on her hips and glared at him. Oddly enough, she was almost relieved to be back on her usual footing with Drew. "Face the facts, Sinclair. You wouldn't recognize an angel if one flew down from heaven and shoved a feather up your nose. I wonder if that's why, for all your arrogant self-righteousness, you still want me after all these years."

The raspiness of her voice was an added and totally unexpected bonus. Drew wasn't to know that it was caused by terror at what she'd just allowed her mouth to say, and not her ability as a femme fatale. But when he reacted physically to the deliberate taunt, satisfaction overcame all fear. She nearly chortled out loud when his chest rose on a swiftly indrawn breath, his teeth clamping together so tightly a muscle throbbed madly against his cheek.

Those silver eyes of his no longer seemed the least bit cold. In fact they were burning her alive, and when his hands grasped her waist she was no longer quite so pleased with herself. Her response to his touch through the thin material of her blouse was shockingly swift and frighteningly intense. She felt as though she were balancing on the edge of a tidal wave and at any moment the towering waters would close over her head.

Maria almost wished they would. She was tired of fighting an attraction that had become an integral part of her life over the years. The thought was startling in its simplicity, but dangerously so. To let herself drown beneath the force of this man's passion might bring temporary euphoria, but it would almost certainly be followed by an eternity of regret. No matter how hard she tried, she would never be able to fit into his life.

There was too much he didn't know about her, too much she never wanted him to know. If he ever found out, he would end up despising her, and she would find herself cast up on a barren shore, more alone than she'd ever been before. She couldn't let that happen, she thought with renewed determination, at least not without one last attempt to save herself.

Maria's head jerked back from its proximity to Drew's with automatic defensiveness. Before he could halt her body's momentum, her skull slammed against the sliding glass door behind her. Wincing at the blow, she glanced up at him with what dignity she had left. Which was woefully little, when she paused long enough to view the childishness of her actions through the pink and white spots floating in front of her eyes.

He frowned and tightened his arms around her. "Are you all right?"

Discomposed by the tingling sensation in her breasts caused by contact with his muscle-hardened chest, she responded to his concerned question with a flippancy she hadn't intended to display. "Don't I feel all right?"

Sighing with understandable impatience, he gave her a shake that made her teeth rattle. "You're teasing the wrong man, Maria."

"I've been the soul of discretion since you came home from Washington," she protested grumpily. "You're the one doing the harassing, and would you please let go of me? I'd like to sit down."

"Then why don't we go over to the couch so we can talk in comfort?" he suggested.

Eyeing him uneasily, she said, "You go ahead. I'm dying for some coffee. Would you like a cup?"

She didn't wait long enough for him to respond. Sidestepping him abruptly, she headed toward the kitchen hurriedly. Drew didn't utter a word of protest when her hair slapped him in the face, because he was too busy watching the sinuous sway of her body. He wondered if she was deliberately swinging that adorably rounded backside of hers in an attempt to fog his thinking processes.

The trouble was, she was succeeding, he realized in disgust. It wasn't a craving for caffeine that was causing his pulse to quicken, and the flesh hardening in his crotch sure wasn't the result of rational thought. But in spite of his self-castigation, his glance slid down her back with compulsive thoroughness as she stood in front of her coffee maker. Her well-worn jeans fit her like a glove, and her dainty blouse was curtained by the silken fall of her hair. Damn, but she made him want to sit up and howl!

Drew remembered getting drunk on the mere sight of her after months of abstinence. He hadn't been home since the previous summer. Thus he'd arrived at the pool party Tricia had given to celebrate his return last month, fully confident that he'd put his obsession with Maria behind him. Then he'd stepped into his sister's backyard and seen Maria poised on the diving board in a figure-hugging white maillot.

Her legs were long and slim for a woman of her diminutive height, and the sight of all that lovely wet skin had caused him to take cold showers several nights running. The self-inflicted punishment hadn't helped to lessen the frequency of the erotic dreams that continued to disturb his sleep, but then a man couldn't expect miracles.

Maria's voice broke into his introspective reveries with grating cheerfulness. "Are you taking root in my carpet, Drew?"

Stepping past him, she busily set a laden tray onto the glass-topped coffee table in front of her couch. With a trembling breath, he inhaled the scent of her, which lingered in the air. The evocative aroma, slightly sweet and floral, was one he associated specifically with Maria. It was all it took to complete his discomposure. As he watched her bend to lift a stoneware carafe from the tray, he felt sweat break out on his forehead as he desperately tried to control his runaway libido.

Six

Maria turned and offered him a large ceramic mug, deliberately avoiding his eyes as she did so. He absentmindedly took a sip and grimaced as he stared down at the dark brew in his hand. He didn't want coffee, he thought with frustrated certainty, he wanted Maria! Just where in the hell was his celebrated decisiveness when he needed it? he asked himself, his sense of grievance advancing by leaps and bounds. Out of all the women he'd known, why was this beautiful black-haired witch the only female capable of reducing him to a sweating mass of confusion?

As Maria lifted her cup to inhale its steamy contents, Drew studied the graceful movements of her arms in abject fascination. Her dusky flesh was smooth and rounded, and he swallowed tightly as a pair of dimpled elbows were exposed to his sight. He reached up to loosen his collar, which seemed unusu-

ally constricting all of a sudden, and felt like a fool
when he discovered the top three buttons at the throat
of his burgundy sport shirt were already unfastened.
But then, he figured that any man who got turned on
by a couple of elbows was already sporting a few
cracker crumbs in his bread basket.

The visual impact Maria made on his senses alone
gave him pleasure. Her dark hair and creamy skin
made a striking contrast against the bone white leather
of the long, deeply cushioned couch. Several colorful
throw pillows on either side of her also warmed what
would otherwise have been a stark decor, as did the
brightly hued mural painted on the far wall. Yet even
as his mind registered these facts, all he could really
think about was how much he wanted to make love to
her.

Maria wasn't faring much better than Drew. The
intensity of his expression was making her nervous
enough to bite off all her fingernails, and it took real
effort to keep her hands away from her mouth. Unable to tell what thoughts were going through his
mind, she wondered if they were as erotically stimu-
lating as her own. He was so beautiful, she thought
dreamily, a golden warrior with the courage to chase
the shadows from his life. So different from her, she
mused, saddened by the realization. She, who spent
her life hiding from the dark specters instead of con-
fronting them.

The fanciful comparison was too painful to con-
template for more than an instant. With studied control she leaned forward and placed her cup down on
the rectangular-shaped glass of the brass-based coffee
table in front of her. Her hand trembled slightly,
sloshing some of the brown liquid into the white-and-

green-patterned saucer, but she managed to smile with commendable brightness as she waved her hand toward a large overstuffed armchair nearby. "Aren't you going to sit down, Drew? You make me nervous, hovering over me like that."

Slowly he walked toward the coffee table, his eyes never leaving hers as he placed his unwanted coffee back onto the tray. "If I hovered over you the way I really want to," he admitted huskily, "you'd really have something to get nervous about. Right now all I can think about is you and me on that couch. I'd strip both of us down to our bare skin and I'd lie on you, and arouse you until you cried out for me to take you."

Her cheeks reddened at the explicitness of his verbal lovemaking. "Will you stop pressuring me into becoming your lover?"

"I've offered to marry you," he reminded her, his voice harsh with censure. "What more do you want from me?"

"I want to be left alone!"

His gaze narrowed on her rebellious features, and the breath burst from his lungs on a turbulent sigh. He moved so swiftly she didn't have time for more than a gasp. Frozen in openmouthed consternation, she felt him grasp her wrists and pull her up in front of him. For an instant she swayed unsteadily, but soon was yanked against his hard body in a contact that seared her from breast to thigh.

She inhaled his warm, coffee-scented breath and experienced an inward melting that completely shattered her defensive system. The heat emanating from him made her weak, and she slumped against him with little poise and even less self-control. Immediately his taut frame began to imprint itself against every inch of her traitorously sensitized flesh. She was left with no doubt as to the extent of his arousal . . . or her own.

"Tell me you don't want this," he demanded, cupping her hipbones and grinding her against his hardening thickness, "Tell me you don't want me!"

What she'd heard about anger sometimes acting as an aphrodisiac must be true, she thought faintly, barely able to stop herself from arching against him. He was so wonderfully close, and she longed to appease the ache growing in her body. Why don't you? a traitorous voice inside of her questioned temptingly. She bit down hard on her lower lip, hoping the pain would bring her to her senses.

Unfortunately, the maneuver only seemed to intensify the desire darkening Drew's eyes. If the implacable expression on his face was any indication, she decided weakly, lying to him would be useless. Shivering with excitement, she realized how much easier it would be to give in to his demands. All she had to do was yield, and the decision would be taken out of her hands.

Not that she had much of a choice. To be honest, she doubted if she had enough strength left for more than an ineffectual whimper of protest. Desire was sapping her will, as though an insidious virus had taken hold of her trembling frame. Her nipples were pouting with embarrassing impertinence and were probably already visible through the well-washed thinness of her blouse. One wriggle or a decent lungful of oxygen, she decided wryly, and voilà, she wouldn't be the only one to feel their pebble hardness!

Once that happened, she hadn't the slightest doubt that he would take full advantage of her weakness. Just the thought made her heart pound against the wall of her chest, and she was shocked to realize that she wasn't at all dismayed at the prospect. It was shyness more than any intrinsic panic that made her take her fate in her own hands. Tentatively at first, and then more forcefully, she began pushing against his rib cage. "Please stop, Drew."

"Why should I?" he muttered, the question muffled against her soft, fragrant neck. "You take a perverse delight in driving me crazy, so why shouldn't I return the compliment?"

"Haven't you ever heard of cause and effect?" she questioned breathlessly. "If you push, I'm going to shove. I'm only human."

He raised his head, and a tiny spark burst to life in his eyes. It definitely wasn't induced by an excess of temper, Maria decided nervously. Slowly his thumbs began probing the hollows between her shoulder and collarbones, his touch sliding the softness of her single garment against her quickening flesh.

"Then maybe it's time I showed you just how human I can be, Maria."

She began shaking like a sapling in a gale-force wind, her ears attuned to the sensuality in his voice. She nearly choked when she tried to swallow and roughly cleared her throat of the tense lump blocking her breathing passage. Straightening her back, she glared at him through lowered lashes. "You continually insult me and then expect to seduce me. What's your problem, Sinclair? Can't you make up your mind?"

"You're my problem, and my mind's been made up regarding you for quite some time."

She plucked furiously at the hands that were now cupped around her neck, her dark eyes sullenly resentful. "You couldn't prove it by me. You haven't been around for quite some time."

A muscle pulsed in his jaw, and the corners of his mouth tightened into a disapproving slant. "Maybe I haven't been ready to deal with the problem until now."

"There's an easy solution to your difficulties, Drew. All you have to do is follow the pattern of the past couple of years and keep away from me."

His fingers tightened at the taunt, causing her to wince and pull away from his touch. "In case I haven't mentioned it," she snapped, "I don't appreciate being mauled. I'm not one of your empty-headed little playthings, and I have no intention of becoming one!"

Two large, beautifully shaped hands were raised into the air in a defensive gesture, and Drew glanced from one to the other with an exaggerated air of surprise. His expression was saintly enough to get him through heaven's pearly gates without a question being asked, Maria thought in disgust. He had the face of an angel and the soul of a devil, an unfair combination if ever there was one. And she was frustrated enough, she acknowledged wrathfully, to snitch Gabriel's horn and blow the whistle on him herself.

A wickedly amused gleam sparked his eyes, and his less than chaste words merely reinforced her thoughts. "When I get around to handling you," he said, his voice rife with laughter, "I promise you won't have the least objection, Gypsy."

"Dream on, Counselor. You might be able to impress lovely bimbos like Delia Lang, but that's only because they don't know you like I do. And don't call me Gypsy," she tacked on for good measure.

"It suits you," he said softly. "You're all flashing eyes and honey gold skin, and you have no idea how badly I want to see every inch of you sprawled naked on top of my sheets."

The mental picture his raspy words created nearly threw her into cardiac arrest, and heat flushed her face as her heart began running away with itself. "You might as well get some pleasure from your imagination, because you'll be the last man to see me sprawled anywhere."

The flash of his smile nearly knocked her to her knees. "Will I?" he murmured.

Dirty pool! Foul! Time out! The silent protests echoed in her mind, but there was no referee to come to her assistance. As she opened her mouth to set him straight, she could only hope that her voice sounded more certain than she felt. "The very... last man, Andrew Sinclair!"

A sardonic grin greeted her breathless denial, but there was a complete lack of irony in his ragged response. "You know, I get hot just wondering if we'll make love as violently as we argue, Maria."

Oh, Lord! This mellow-voiced, seductive stranger was not the chiding, sharp-tongued man she'd come to know and hate. She was thrown off balance by his change in tactics, and was more than slightly leery of his practiced charm. Although both bewildered and suspicious, she could suddenly understand why women chased him with such disgusting eagerness. Now that he'd decided to aim all that male sensuality in her direction, she was proving to be a gullible, wide-eyed female.

Maybe even more so than most, she decided crossly, but surely a healthy sense of self-preservation would prevent her from succumbing to the sensuous spell he was trying to cast over her? Not entirely convinced she was right, she tilted her chin in a haughty gesture of dismissal. "Then you'd better find some way to cool off, because you're not talking me into your bed."

"Is that a challenge?" he questioned gently.

If she wasn't already barefoot, that confident, intense note in his voice would have had her shaking in her shoes. Instantly her head whipped from side to side in a rapidly negative gesture that nearly threw her neck out of joint. This time she was going to quit while she was ahead. She might often be impetuous, maybe even a little reckless on occasion, she accepted ruefully, but she wasn't completely off her trolley. This man could chew her up and spit her out long before she even realized he'd taken a bite.

That certainty made her stammer a timely if somewhat cowardly retraction. "I . . . I didn't mean to . . ."

Her mouth quivered as her words trailed off into an uneasy silence, and Drew's lips parted as though attempting to absorb the taste of her through osmosis. He was sick of denying himself because of foolish pride, tired of pretending he didn't want this beautiful little temptress like hell on fire. *Before this night is over, a certain black-eyed gypsy is going to admit she belongs to me and no other man,* he vowed with inwardly fierce determination. And the sooner he achieved that goal, he thought, the better it would be for both of them.

His voice hoarse with suppressed emotion, he asked, "Were you going to deny challenging me, Maria? Haven't you realized by now that your very existence is a challenge?"

"I can't help the way you react to me," she whispered.

"I'm not asking you to," he stated bluntly. "All I want is honesty in our relationship from now on. We have too many walls between us that don't need to be there, and I want them torn down."

She pressed her trembling fingers against the ache beginning to throb in her temples. Gazing at him with sadly haunted eyes, she uttered a plaintive cry. "We don't have a relationship, Drew. There can't be honesty without trust, and almost from the beginning you've gone out of your way to doubt every word I've said."

"I'm not denying my part in building some of those walls I mentioned." Grimacing wryly, he ran impatient fingers through his hair. "I hated the way you made me feel, and lying to myself was one way of fighting the attraction."

Lowering his arms, he shoved his hands into the back pockets of his jeans and shrugged dismissively. "At first I told myself you were too young, and later I tried convincing myself that you weren't the type of woman I admired. But in reality I was running scared, Maria. I couldn't get you out from under my skin, and I didn't want any woman having that kind of hold on me."

"You still don't, but you'd like to gain such an advantage over me," she accused him bitterly. "You talk about making love, but for all your experience you don't know the meaning of the word. All you've learned is how to use women for your own satisfaction, and I have too much respect for myself to let that happen to me.''

Another small fragment of the puzzle that was Maria slotted into place in his mind, and he stared at the woman before him in shamed realization. Recent discoveries had shown him she wasn't the shallow, thoughtless dilettante of his imagination, and now he acknowledged depths to her personality he'd never bothered to plumb. Her words held a degree of understanding he'd never seen, mainly because it was a quality he hadn't wanted to find.

Guilt ate at his insides as he realized just how great his injustice to her had been. She was a warm, intelligent woman, capable of an unusual degree of compassion. Whether founding an organization to aid the homeless or taking two children into her home to provide them with the security they needed, she gave of herself without counting the cost. Just as she had to Phelps, he thought in painful realization, a man who had earned her love and devotion. Drew knew he had been too stupidly satisfied with the false image of her he'd built in his mind to try to meet her on equal ground, but he was no longer willing to hide from reality where Maria was concerned.

Now he'd come full circle, and he knew he would do almost anything to have her. She had done her share of hiding the truth about herself from him, but what he needed to know was why. What made her avoid him so assiduously, and why did she continue to deny the attraction between them? Usually he was the one who had to do the avoiding. He had a great deal to offer a woman, he thought without conceit, but Maria wasn't impressed by his wealth or his social status. Her re-

fusal of his proposal had convinced him of that, he
decided wryly. Then what in hell could he offer her
that she might want?

The answer slammed him in the gut with the force
of a two-by-four as he realized that he'd never given
Maria his respect. Lust, contempt and possessiveness
he'd offered in plenty, because it had been safer to
convince himself that those were the only emotions she
merited from him. The truth was unpalatable, but it
was something he was going to have to face if he hoped
to untangle the knotted threads of their relationship.

Oh, he had wanted her all right, but only on the pe-
riphery of his life! In reality he'd been terrified of letting her get close to him, and had hidden his emotional
cowardice behind a defensive, disdainful shield. He
had strengthened that shield by turning his own self-
disgust outward, and she had been forced to retaliate
in order to maintain her dignity.

He knew she was as drawn to him as he was to her,
if only physically, but that was a pretty big "if." It said
a great deal for the strength of her character that she
had bothered to fight him, especially when for years
he'd been more than willing to take the easy way out
and let her own deceptions go unchallenged. Was it
any wonder, he asked himself, that she had learned to
hold him in contempt?

He despised himself at that moment, but revealed
none of his unease as he utilized the only advantage of
which he could be certain. "You can pretend indifference to me, but I don't think you can make yourself
believe it. Even before Phelps died, it was me you
wanted in your bed, Gypsy."

At his reference to Tom, all the old resentment that
she'd held inside for so long burst free, and she knew

she could no longer continue the deception. "Don't you dare say another word," she demanded with suppressed violence. "Not one more word! When you asked me to leave Tom and go to Washington to live with you, it wasn't marriage you offered me. You may have only thought me good enough to qualify as a mistress, but Tom was a wonderful man who loved me. He sacrificed himself to teach me my value as a human being, and he did so without asking for a single thing in return. I owe him more than I can ever repay, and I'm sick of you slandering our relationship!"

Drew stiffened in shock, his features whitening as he whispered, "You were never his mistress, were you?"

"Of course I wasn't," she snapped angrily. "Tom was like a father to me."

"Then why let me go on thinking . . . ?"

"The worst?" she questioned with a cynical smile. "Wasn't that what you wanted, Drew, to have me without any strings? But taking your sister's best friend to bed would have provided plenty, so in your mind you made me into the kind of woman you could seduce without having your conscience bother you."

A dull flush colored his cheekbones as he nodded curtly in agreement. "I'm sorry for hurting you, but I'm even more ashamed of sullying your foster father's good name. He must have been quite a man, Maria. I wish I'd taken the opportunity to get to know him when I had the chance."

"He was," she admitted pensively, her thoughts full of the one person in her life she had trusted unconditionally. "You want to know why I've always refused to discuss my past openly, Drew? You try going through life as a number on a welfare register, and you'd understand the stigma attached to that kind of existence. Before Tom came along I was dragged from one foster home to another, like some poor, recalcitrant mongrel on a leash. He was the one who saved me from strangling to death.''

Although he winced at the vividness of her analogy, he still attempted a defensive reminder in his favor. ''That's more than you've ever willingly told me about yourself, do you realize that? Oh, I knew you were orphaned as a child, but I had to badger Tricia into telling me that much. When I first met you you seemed so shy and sweet, I used to watch you and curse myself for wanting you.''

At her startled expression he laughed, but the sound held only mockery. ''Yes, even then I ached to have you,'' he admitted hollowly. ''I felt like a lecher lusting after a schoolgirl, until after that damned party you and Tricia sneaked off to attend. I went to your place to apologize for yelling at you, and was confronted by a seductive vision in black satin and lace.

''Damn it, Maria! After that what in the hell was I supposed to think? You threw me completely off balance, shrouding yourself in mystery and deflecting every question I ever asked about your background. I've had to wade through a conspiracy of silence to get to you, even with my own sister. I've taken bits and pieces and tried to fit them together into a cohesive whole, but without much success. Was it any wonder that I reached all the wrong conclusions?''

She bit her lip and averted her gaze. ''No,'' she murmured guiltily.

''Then why couldn't you have been honest with me?''

A storm of emotion suddenly raged in her eyes. ''Just because Tricia and I were close and she confided in you, did it automatically follow that I was obligated to do the same? The logical part of my brain knew I wasn't to blame for my upbringing, but that didn't prevent me from being ashamed of my lack of parentage. You were already contemptuous of me, and I wasn't about to give you more ammunition to use against me. I had a right to privacy, Drew.''

Her words were razor sharp, painful but necessary to deflate the masculine ego she'd railed against on so many occasions. Drew was forced to view the past through her eyes, and he didn't much like what he saw. Being so much in the public eye, he was a man who guarded his own privacy zealously. Why then had he condemned her for doing the same?

After a thoughtful pause he inhaled deeply and studied her tense features with brooding eyes. ''Yes, you had a right to privacy. Only that wasn't the real issue between us then, and it certainly isn't now, Maria. You judged me and found me wanting, without really giving me a chance to prove myself worthy of your trust.''

''Why should I have bothered?''

This time there was a definite hint of sadness behind the slant of his mouth. ''For the same reason I'm here with you now,'' he replied quietly.

This was the first of those walls he'd referred to earlier, she realized, and he was silently asking her to remove the first stone. To do so would be an admission of sorts, a weakening of her internal defenses. Did she want to eliminate any more barriers between them? Did she dare lower her guard and risk the pain that would almost certainly result from a more intimate relationship with this man?

Friendship was one thing, but he was asking for more. Could she give him what he wanted, what they both wanted, she corrected honestly, without losing a vital part of herself in the process? She was unable or, more accurately, unwilling to unbury certain shameful aspects of her past. Yet that didn't mean she couldn't take a first step in reaching a closer understanding with Drew, did it? As long as she remembered the reasons why they could never be more than lovers, surely it would be safe to store up a few golden memories for a future spent without him?

Hesitantly she began to speak, her voice subdued. "What you said earlier, well . . . you were right. I was less than honest with you, because I didn't know how to handle the attraction between us. You have to understand that growing up the way I did, I saw too many girls who let themselves be used by men in an attempt to gain the love and approval they craved."

She lowered her gaze to the floor and quivered as she wrapped her arms around her chest in a defensive posture. "When you kissed me that first time I was terrified of the things you made me feel, so I made certain you wouldn't want to repeat the experience. It was easier to fuel your disgust, than it would have been for me to overcome my own insecurities."

Slowly he reached out and cupped her cheeks in his hands, a warm, tender light in his eyes as he forced her head up. "Then from here on out we're going to take some time to get to know each other, Maria. We've got more than a strong physical attraction going for us. If it were just sex I craved, I could appease that appetite elsewhere."

He laughed as her cheeks again grew rosy, and bent his head to place a teasing kiss against the tip of her nose. "It's taken me a long time to accept the fact that other women have only whetted my appetite for you, but I want a chance to prove I can be more than just a satisfactory bed partner. What I propose is that we put aside our sensual cravings for a while, and get on with the business of friendship. I may crowd you a bit, but I promise not to push you too far, too fast. Have we got a deal, Gypsy?"

Maria couldn't have denied him anything at that moment, and suddenly even the hated nickname brought an odd leap of joy to her heart.

Seven

"**A**re you ready to go, honey?"

Maria stuffed the last letter into its corresponding envelope and looked up at Drew with a tired smile. "I have to sort these letters into the bags the post office provided and lock up before I can leave."

The short, frizzy gray curls of her assistant manager at Hidden Creek, one of the most steadfast FACES volunteers, went into motion beside her. "You leave the locking up to me," her motherly voice scolded. "You haven't gotten out of this place before midnight all week, and you're exhausted. If you're not careful you're going to make yourself sick, and I'm too busy right now to visit you in the hospital."

A pair of snapping brown eyes passed over Maria as if she had all the substantiality of a gnat, and rose to the man standing behind her. "Get her home before she collapses, and make her take it easy this weekend,

Drew. The rest of us will bag up this lot for the mail pickup on Monday.''

Marge's plump arm gestured to the few diehards left in the large warehouse that served as FACES headquarters, and he nodded in agreement. ''I'll bring the car around front, Marge. Just make sure this stubborn woman doesn't start on anything else while I'm gone.''

Ignoring Maria's petulant scowl of protest, he turned on his heel and exited the building with a disgusting degree of energy. She noted the swiftness of his footsteps as he crossed the scarred wooden floor and wondered if the man ever got tired. Just watching him move wore her out, but the realization didn't surprise her. For the past few weeks nearly all of their free time had been spent together, and she'd rapidly come to realize that not many men possessed Andrew Sinclair's reserves of strength.

Once that clever brain of his devised a course of action he became a human dynamo, and as tenacious as a bulldog. Which made her wonder at the easy, undemanding companion he'd become. As he had promised, not by word or deed had he attempted to coax her into his bed. He avoided being alone with her, and the hours they spent together were filled with activity.

They'd dined at some of the Bay Area's most exclusive restaurants, she'd been coaxed down the waterslides at Shadow Cliffs in Livermore, and he'd even bullied her into taking a ride in a glider. They had spent an entire day and evening at the Santa Cruz boardwalk, and another day touring Fisherman's Wharf and Ghirardelli Square in San Francisco. She

hadn't realized that getting to know Drew would prove
so exhausting.

He had also become a familiar figure at FACES
headquarters, and had thrown himself into his volunteer work with a boundless enthusiasm that had
seemed to rejuvenate everyone around him. At first his
involvement had been a means to an end. Maria
hadn't been willing to neglect her responsibilities, and
Drew hadn't been satisfied with the small amount of
time she was able to put aside to spend with him.

As he had so succinctly put it, "If you can't beat
'em, join 'em." So he had rolled up his sleeves and
plunged into the fray, and with increasing frequency
more and more FACES members were going to him
for advice. His knowledge of the law was proving to
be invaluable and his contacts in the business world a
godsend. He had already implemented several pro-
grams aimed at generating new revenue, and because
of his professional reputation and his influence with
the news media, FACES finances were healthier than
ever before.

A small smile tugged at the corners of her mouth as
she collected her purse from the floor. Between his
thriving law practice and his volunteer work here, was
it any wonder that poor Drew had practically forgotten his seduction techniques? Her smile slipped a
notch, and a familiar sense of irritation rose inside of
her. Much to her disgust, she didn't find the thought
at all amusing.

In fact, she was becoming increasingly resentful of
his preoccupation with the new challenges in his life.
Ever since the night of their pact, his behavior toward
her could be likened to that of a brother. Unfortunately, she'd never wanted the dratted man as a sib-

ling! Tricia might be over the moon at their new camaraderie, but Maria was definitely reserving judgment.

"My, but that man gives me palpitations!"

Maria's faltering smile was given a rejuvenating shot in the arm, and she glanced at her assistant manager in mock disapproval. "You're a great-grandmother!"

Marge's impressive bosom expanded as she inhaled, and the toss of her head set her permed curls to bouncing. "Now, don't you get sassy with me, missy. Just because a poor old widow woman becomes a great-grandma, it doesn't automatically follow that she ends up paralyzed from the neck down. There's life in the old gal yet."

"You're right," Maria agreed meekly. "I forgot all about the gossip you caused at the Pleasanton fair last month."

Marge's plump cheeks sported two brilliant red spots, and the bodice of her print dress began to heave like a bellows. "It wasn't my idea for that old fool Eckersly to buy two dozen tickets."

Maria had been treated to the wicked arch of Drew's eyebrows too many times to resist imitating him, and her friend now received the result of the hours she'd practiced in front of her bathroom mirror. "No one forced you to volunteer to man the kissing booth."

Marge's large cocker spaniel eyes widened innocently. "I seem to remember Tricia trying to get you to do it, but you opted for the cakewalk instead. Somebody had to take up the slack."

Marge snorted with amusement when Maria suddenly became busy rearranging the contents of her purse. "You knew darned good and well that Drew would have bought every ticket going before he'd have let any other man kiss you.''

"He would not," she retorted, her lips pursing primly. "He doesn't have bottomless pockets."

"How would you know?" Marge chortled gleefully. "You never get close enough to the man's pants to find out."

Maria felt heat scorching her own cheeks, and the sudden strident blaring of a car horn provided a welcome reprieve. "That's Drew," she stated unnecessarily, her movements flustered as she turned in the direction of the sound. "See you later, Marge."

A snide cackle greeted her hasty retreat, and Maria was still struggling to subdue her embarrassment as she slid into Drew's black BMW. She could feel his gaze on her as she did up her seat belt, and she grew more disgruntled by the minute. Reaching out, he ran his knuckles down the scarlet cheek nearest him. His voice quivered with amusement as he said, "You look as if someone ruffled your feathers, little bird. What's the matter, has Marge been teasing you again?"

"She's not alone," she muttered petulantly. "Everyone seems to be taking potshots at me lately. They all think I'm crazy for not snapping you up while I have the chance, especially after you started spouting all that garbage about wanting to settle down with the right woman. I could box your ears for causing me so many headaches, Drew Sinclair!"

He assumed an innocent expression, and she ground her teeth together as he gave a shrug of his broad shoulders. "I have Charlie's blessing."

She slanted him a pointed glare and crossed her arms over her chest as she slumped in her seat. "I don't know how you managed to hoodwink him, but he's beginning to think you walk on water. In fact," she muttered in a disgruntled voice, "so does everyone else."

His laughter accompanied the muted roar of the engine as he accelerated into the street, and Maria refused to utter another word all the way home. She was more than just tired, she realized. A niggling sense of dissatisfaction was making her life miserable, and she no longer knew what she wanted. Drew's behavior toward her couldn't be faulted, and yet she perversely missed the taunting, sensually riveting devil who used to inhabit his body. Her reaction wasn't rational, but neither were the erotic dreams that had lately begun to disturb her normal sleep pattern.

Surprised by a yawn, she twisted in Drew's direction and rubbed her cheek against the leather headrest of the luxurious car's bucket seat. Her eyes closed automatically, and her body grew slack as a pleasant haze dulled her mind. Another yawn followed the first, and with a kittenish murmur she gave in to the need for rest. Her last thoughts were centered around a pair of wicked gray eyes and a smile beguiling enough to make the angels plead for mercy.

Stopping at a signal light, the man at her side slid his eyes over her relaxed features. As his glance continued downward his fingers clenched around the steering wheel, his knuckles whitening from the tightness of his grip. Her green-and-gold-patterned peasant skirt had ridden up until it barely covered her thighs, and the sight of all that bare, rounded flesh made him realize he'd reached the end of the road.

He'd waited for Maria with a patience he hadn't known he possessed, but tonight he wouldn't be leaving her at her door like a good little Boy Scout. She had learned he could be a friend, and now he was ready to have her learn to accept him as a lover. If he'd gauged the reason for her recent, uncharacteristic moodiness, he thought with a satisfied grin, she was more than ready to take the next step in their relationship.

If she had glanced at him in that instant, her initial reassurance would have quickly deteriorated into panic-stricken certainty—because Drew's smile held all the devilishness she'd earlier desired, and his silver eyes were smoldering with a heat to rival that in Hades.

Eight

Maria blinked sleepily as she fumbled to fit her key into the lock, her eyes watering as she tried focusing on the door. With a muffled laugh, Drew took the key from her and pushed her hands aside. "Here, let me do that."

Her thank-you was muffled as she braced herself against a convenient wall, and another chuckle shook him as he told her, "You remind me of a baby owl, all bleary-eyed and ruffled feathers. You should have let me carry you from the car like I wanted to. At least then you wouldn't have had to wake up completely."

Disgruntled by his teasing, she muttered, "And let you put me to bed? Not likely, Sinclair."

"Ah, the little fledgling pecks when she's tired." As he taunted her he threw open the door, and she stumbled through the opening with an irritated, stiff-legged gait. "Do you have a bird fetish or something? This is the second time you've compared me to one."

After following her inside and flicking on the hall light, he turned and locked the door. Hearing the click of the dead bolt, she swiveled around with a heartbeat to rival Thumper's. When she remembered that Thumper had been a lovesick little bunny rabbit in the Walt Disney animated classic *Bambi,* the moisture in her mouth disappeared like magic. Well, she wasn't lovesick, she decided staunchly. Not at all, no way, no sirree!

Much to her consternation, Drew chose that moment to reach for her. Her thoughts scattered as he pulled her against his warm body. One hand lifted to the braid coiled against the back of her slender neck, and he smiled as he began to free her thick hair from its confinement. "A bird fetish?" he inquired wickedly. "Are you wondering if I like my sex kinky?"

"I'm wondering what you think you're doing?" she retorted belligerently.

His husky laugh caused her to shiver as her body absorbed the vibrations through her pores. "I'm helping you to get ready for bed," he said matter-of-factly.

"I can get to bed on my own." With a saccharin smile, she said, "Drive carefully on the way home, Drew."

Although the expression on his face remained gentle, there was an implacable gleam in his eyes. "It's been hours since we've eaten. Why don't you shower and change while I fix us a snack?"

She was so relieved when he released her and turned in the direction of the kitchen, she bit back the protest forming in her mind. Let him be bossy and dictatorial, she thought grumpily, as long as it kept his hands busy and his mind off fetishes. Spinning on her heels, she stomped off down the hall. She slammed her bedroom door for good measure, gritting her teeth when she once again heard his hearty laugh ring out.

After a brief shower, she wrapped a towel around herself and tended to her hair. It was slightly damp from the bathroom mist, but since it had been washed that morning it didn't resist the ministrations of her brush. Which was a good thing, since she was too tired to spend any time on it now. Once it was lying smoothly over her shoulders, she returned to her bedroom and headed for her dresser.

She quickly donned a pair of black lace bikini panties and walked over to her closet. Pulling an ankle-length caftan off a padded hanger, she sighed with pleasure as the cool, silky fabric slid over her head and brushed against her bare flesh. She had several similar lounging gowns in bright, cheerful colors, but this was her favorite. The bodice was formfitting and cut in a deep vee, and the loose quarter-length sleeves gave her a feeling of freedom. She smiled cockily as she caught sight of her reflection in the mirror, thoroughly approving of the way the dark emerald green material complemented her pale olive complexion.

Although refreshed and more alert than she'd been half an hour ago, there was still a petulant slant to her mouth as she joined Drew in the kitchen. He was standing in front of the stove with a towel tied around his waist, and he was so gorgeous she was tempted to make a grab for him. The urge did nothing to improve her mood. When he looked her up and down in masculine appreciation and uttered a wolf whistle, she responded to his implied approval with a self-conscious frown. "I'm not hungry," she snapped grouchily.

He studied her surreptitiously as he began to set dishes and cutlery on the table, and struggled to suppress a grin. She looked adorable with her flushed cheeks and that disgruntled pout to her mouth, and he ignored her protest with the ease of long practice. Grabbing the omelet pan from the stove, he wafted it under her nose. "Not even a little hungry?"

Since the delectable aroma of egg, spices and cheese made her stomach rumble quite audibly, she plopped down into the kitchen chair in defeat. "Sometimes I hate you."

"I know," he murmured soothingly, sliding half of the omelet onto her plate with a dexterous flick of his wrist. "Go ahead and start eating while I butter the toast. Do you want juice or milk with your meal?"

Not wanting to show undue eagerness, she carefully placed her napkin in her lap before lifting her fork. "I want coffee."

Since his head was safely stuck in the bowels of the refrigerator, he allowed himself a smile at her plaintive response. "Coffee will keep you awake."

A loud yawn greeted his statement. "Nothing will keep me awake."

Oh, yeah? As he visualized all the ways he planned to occupy her time for the rest of the night, a surge of heat enveloped his loins. Clearing his throat to stop himself from groaning, he slammed the refrigerator door shut and crossed to the opposite side of the kitchen. Knowing by the hardening of his body that it would be wiser to avoid facing her for a while, he busied himself with the coffee maker. "All right, but one's your limit."

Maria ended up drinking three cups of the strong, dark liquid. Drew not only failed to object, he never even noticed. He was too fascinated watching her eat, wondering how such a tiny body could do away with so much food. She polished off her omelet, what remained of his when he'd finished and two pieces of toast in short order. "I thought you weren't hungry?" he remarked as he followed her into the living room.

Curling up against the corner of her couch, she gave him a contented smile. "I lied."

Seating himself next to her hips, he whispered, "Like you lied about not wanting me to put you to bed?"

Alarm bells clanged in her mind, and she shifted uneasily. He was back, the smooth-tongued devil with the sexy eyes, and she decided she was crazy to have imagined for one moment that she missed him. He made her skin prickle and her heart race, and she'd probably end up breaking out in a rash if she didn't put some distance between them.

With a dexterity that would have amazed her if she'd taken the time to think about it, she scooted back until she was nearly buried by soft, yielding pillows. "Why d-don't we go out on the deck for a while?" she suggested nervously. "It's such a lovely night, and I need some . . ."

The air she needed was jerked from her lungs in a whoosh as he pulled her against his chest. "You need me, sweet thing."

It was all too true, but she didn't want to admit it. For weeks he'd been directing her every move, interfering in her life, using bullying tactics to get his own way, and he'd done so without indicating any romantic interest in her. And she'd tried her best to tempt him, dammit! Well, enough was enough. How dare he think he could put her down and pick her up like a windup doll? she asked herself, as crabby as any other thwarted woman would be under these circumstances. If he'd gained the impression that it was up to him to decide when they would make love, then she'd just have to show him how wrong he was.

With a toss of her head, she responded to his remark in a voice dripping with sarcasm. "And if I don't need you?"

"You won't be able to help yourself," he said huskily. "I'll please you in ways you've only dreamed about, Gypsy."

"You certainly suffer from more than your share of conceit," she mumbled self-consciously.

"No, but I'm confident of myself as a lover, and I have a very reliable imagination."

The smile that had accompanied his outrageous remark disappeared suddenly, his eyes growing somber as he gazed down at the woman he held pressed to his heart. "You feel like a captured wild thing in my hands, all delicate bones and big dark eyes. Stop shaking, little one. Don't you know I'd never hurt anything as lovely as you?"

Maria was mesmerized by the growled promise and intrigued by the sense of inevitability she felt. "I'm not afraid of you." No, she was afraid of herself, she realized, hearing the shattered quaver in her voice without surprise.

"Good, I'm glad you're through fighting me."

She began to struggle, his smug complacency a new source of irritation. "Like hell I am!"

"You'll be fighting yourself in the end, Maria. After all, I'm only behaving with boring predictability," he continued with a quick, devastatingly impish grin. "You've been waiting for me to jump your bones for weeks, and when I failed to live up to your expectations you turned into a sharp-tongued little shrew. It's time I relieved all that frustration you've been bottling inside, and sweetened you up a bit."

The way he hovered over her made her feel smaller and more ineffectual than usual, and she pushed her chin forward, resistance in every slender line of her body. He might be physically superior, she admitted grudgingly, but she was damned if she was going to cower here like a mouse waiting for the devouring jaws of a hungry cat.

"If you're through amusing me with your Incredible Hulk imitation," she snapped, "I'd like to get up now."

Her sarcasm hit a nerve, and his body went rigid. A muscle pulsed out of control beneath the tight skin covering his jawline, the softness of his voice more threatening than if he'd shouted at her. "Since you find me so amusing, maybe I should give you something else to laugh about."

Even before he finished speaking, his body inclined toward hers with the balletic swiftness of superb conditioning. With a muffled cry she recoiled in alarm, only to freeze in confusion when she noticed the startled look in his eyes. Along with the surprise she saw in their depths was a flicker of anguish at her instinctive rejection.

His voice held unmistakable pain as he whispered, "Haven't these weeks together changed anything be-

tween us, honey? Will you never stop pulling away
from me?''

"I...I didn't mean to," she admitted brokenly.
"I...you make me nervous."

"Do I?"

When she nodded jerkily, his features softened with
tenderness. He reached out to brush back her hair, his
hand exquisitely gentle as he smoothed a few rebellious strands from her moist temple. His chest expanded as he touched her, and she felt her own lungs
fill with an accompanying breath. Their gazes joined
for a brief, vibrantly intense moment, while his fingertips caressed the contour of her head with studied
care.

His thick, blunt-tipped lashes lowered to form dark
crescents beneath his eyelids, as though he felt the
need to shield his innermost thoughts from her. With
eyes shut tight he grasped her thick black hair in both
hands and carefully lifted the long, flowing strands
away from the back of her neck. She heard his
breathing slow and deepen revealingly, until the air
emerged from his lungs with audible difficulty.

The labored rasp seemed to disturb him as much as
it did her, because his lips instantly tightened into a
controlled slash. Maria glanced down at the fingers
still entwined in her hair and watched with numb fascination as they flexed repeatedly. He was oddly preoccupied as he slid the shiny onyx tresses forward over
her right shoulder, and she wondered what thoughts
were running through his mind as he arranged them to
his satisfaction.

His contented sigh caught her attention, and her
eyes quickly renewed their inventory of his arresting
features. His mouth was no longer set sternly, a quiz-

zical smile having reformed its tense outline. Frowning with growing uneasiness, she tried once again to gauge his strange mood. Yet his lashes remained lowered, an effective barrier for his emotions. Her voice colored with bewilderment, she whispered his name.

Although his eyes opened obligingly, he merely shook his head while his gaze devoured every inch of her flushed features. Meeting the brooding intensity of his stare provided her with no answers, only more questions and an all-pervading sense of unreality. Then, with an abruptness she found shocking, he cupped her heavy rope of hair between his palms and began to slide his hands down the captured mass.

His expression was blatantly sensual as the back of his knuckles brushed against the soft swell of her breast, and she gasped at the burning sensation that lingered from his touch. The small space separating them became charged with the invisible, yet no less powerful, sexual impulses sizzling between them. She knew she should be protesting against this enforced intimacy, but her tongue seemed to be stuck to the roof of her mouth. She knew she should move away from him, but she couldn't get her body to obey the dictates of her brain.

"Don't," she finally managed to whisper.

A flame smoldered into life in his eyes, and his hands tightened around her hair. Then he muttered something beneath his breath and lifted the ends of the rich, silken bounty to his face. Inhaling deeply, he smiled through the parting strands with singular sweetness. "You smell of sunshine and flowers."

The gruffly voiced statement caused her to stammer with embarrassment. "I...it's my herbal shampoo."

She flinched visibly at the inaneness of the remark, and her disgusted expression caused him to utter a deep-throated chuckle. "Do you smell like this all over?"

If he had asked her if she blushed all over he would have been closer to the mark, she thought, her embarrassment increasing until every inch of flesh on her body felt scorched. "That's none of your business," she retorted primly.

Another burst of laughter greeted her words, and the sound rippled over her skin with breathtaking effect. Yet his amusement revived her resistance, and she pulled away from his restraining hands with an impatiently muttered imprecation. But maneuvering for her release proved to be a grave miscalculation. As soon as his hands were free, he put them to good use by grasping her shoulders and using his superior strength to force her into a reclining position against the couch.

"Oh, no you don't," she spluttered indignantly. "You let me up this instant!"

Devilish lights danced in his silvery eyes. "I'm only making you more comfortable."

Before she had a chance to tell him what she thought of his bullying tactics, her neck was resting against the rounded arm of the couch and he was bending over her. Hating the apparent submissiveness of her position, her vivid eyes flashed a warning. Yet her wordless resistance only seemed to cause him further amusement, and pushing against the hard wall of his chest accomplished nothing.

Nearly seething with frustration, she satisfied herself with a verbal assault. "This has gone far enough, you big oaf. Get off me!"

Drew didn't pay the slightest bit of attention to her demand. He was too enthralled with the stark contrast of jet black hair against supple white leather, his gaze following the rippling cascade until it brushed against the rose-colored carpet. "Do you know how many of my fantasies have been spun around this crowning glory of yours?" he murmured almost absentmindedly.

As her eyes widened in startled realization, he deliberately held her glance. "This is the way I've imagined it a thousand times, all loose and tousled and beautifully sensual. But in my dreams it's flowing over my naked body, and brushing softly against my skin like black velvet."

With a few graphic words he had explained away his earlier preoccupation with her hair, but Maria would rather have remained in ignorance. Such a glimpse into his private fantasies shook her to her soul, and she grew flustered as she wondered just how she was supposed to react to his verbal love play. It was already impossible for her to meet his eyes. She certainly didn't trust herself to speak. Right now her mind had turned to mush, and she doubted if she could think up one single coherent sentence.

Indeed, she was entirely too busy trying to free herself of the image just planted in her brain. She saw a golden-skinned man sprawled across a floral-sheeted mattress, which was framed by white wicker. His muscular body, so long and lean and hard, was covered by a woman who wore raven hair and nothing else. Recognizing the room she'd just pulled out of her subconscious, she gave a dismayed moan. She was nonplussed by the vividness of her imagination, which had placed Drew Sinclair square in the center of her own bed.

Instantly his heated gaze took note of the blood that suffused her cheeks with hectic color. "Of course," he added, as though reading her mind, "in my erotic imaginings you're a bit underdressed yourself. A sexy Lady Godiva with me as her mount."

Maria didn't know where to look to avoid those knowing eyes of his, and she finally settled on a point midway between his strong, forceful chin and the hollow of his tanned throat. She arranged her features into what she hoped was an expression of prim distaste and attempted an amused laugh. "Really, Drew," she exclaimed with a scornful curl of her lush lips. "You'd better assume more control over your imagination. You've got the wrong woman sharing your fantasy life."

"I've got the right woman," he corrected her softly, possessiveness in his low tones. "You have all the fire and wanton beauty of a Gypsy queen, Maria. My Gypsy queen!"

His words served to harden her resolve, and the look she shot him from beneath her lashes was filled with rebellion. "I belong to myself and no one else."

He shifted his upper torso until he was practically lying on top of her, and a jean-clad thigh pressed against her hip. She withdrew from his overpowering closeness as far as she could, but her progress was impeded by the colorful throw pillows piled haphazardly against the back of the couch. She grew even more restricted when a brawny arm braced itself beside her head, the long, graceful fingers of his hand brushing her cheek.

Her petulant features caused that impish sparkle to reappear in his eyes. "Don't you know the time has come for surrender?" he asked with a wry grin.

Trying to gain more breathing room by squirming only caused her to sink deeper into the cushioned corner he'd backed her into, and the look of smug satisfaction on his face made her itch to smack him. Grinding her teeth together until her jaw ached, she gave him a fulminating glare from beneath the thick fringe of her lashes. "In a pig's eye, Sinclair!"

"You aren't being very nice to me, my darling."

"I don't feel very nice," she muttered, "and don't call me darling."

"Why? You are a darling."

"I am not!" Realizing the trap he'd set for her, she uttered a disgruntled sniff, "I mean, I'm not yours."

"But you are." He began to string a series of tiny, nibbling kisses along the delicate curve of her jaw, his voice thickening as he murmured, "Give me a few minutes, and I'll convince you I'm right."

His hotly whispered promise caught her unprepared, and her voice wavered as she rejected his offer. "Not if I can help it. I don't want to be your darling, or your Gypsy queen, or your anything! Can't you get that through that hard head of yours?"

"My head isn't all that's hard," he retorted mockingly, "and my body is urging me to change your mind."

And hers was urging her to let him, she acknowledged honestly, the realization increasing her sense of helplessness. She was being tossed helter-skelter by her emotions, and she hated feeling so out of control. Deciding on sarcasm as her best defense, she said,

"Give your body a good talking to and leave mine alone."

The look he gave her held an oddly touching hint of vulnerability. "Don't you think I've tried talking myself out of this damned obsession I have for you? God, the past few years I've missed you so much, Maria. You don't know how many times I regretted leaving my law practice to accept that political appointment in Washington," he admitted huskily. "Even fighting with you was better than existing without you."

The revealing comment deepened her confusion, and her inner self screamed a resounding, No! The protest echoed in her mind, reigniting the panicked certainty of her own vulnerability. She didn't want him reaching inside of her and discovering the full depth of her own loneliness. He had no right to search out the woman she'd managed to keep hidden from every other man. Such knowledge would give him the strength to defeat her and make it impossible for her to control her desire for him.

"I'm sorry," she replied stiltedly, averting her gaze. "That's not my problem."

Drew stiffened with resentment as she turned her head away from his seeking eyes. For the love of Pete, he thought on an upsurge of pain. Why wouldn't she open up to him? His features coldly condemning, he grasped her chin and forced her to look at him. "The devil you say," he ground out angrily. "Why do you persist in running away from our relationship?"

"I've told you before, we have no relationship," she corrected insistently.

"Then let's call it good, old-fashioned lust and be done with it," he snapped. "You may not want me disturbing your safe, complacent little world, but you sure as hell want me in your bed, woman!''

Maria twisted restlessly, her voice reflecting the trembling of her body. "I don't...I don't want you."

The moment the denial was uttered, she knew she'd gone too far. Drew inhaled sharply, his eyes glittering spears of accusation. She couldn't avoid that encompassing glance, any more than she could prevent his unnatural stillness from accelerating her heartbeat into a thunderous roar. His voice, when it sounded, held the confidence of a man used to taking responsibility for his actions. "Then I'll just have to change your mind," he said thickly. "Heaven knows I've waited long enough to take what's mine."

His head swooped in a downward arc as he spoke, his mouth slanting over hers with demanding force. Her lips parted on a gasp, and he quickly took advantage of the opening she had unwittingly provided for him. His tongue bathed the inner tissue of her lips before seeking a deeper tasting, and she felt every single bone in her body become instantly pliant.

Her ability to resist was gone, but resistance was no longer her top priority. The only things that seemed important were the hands lowering the neckline of her caftan and the gentle fingers brushing the burgeoning fullness of her breasts. The moan that escaped from her throat was captured by the mouth giving her pleasure, and she in turn tasted his answering groan of arousal.

Drew lifted his head and gazed down at the bounty his hands had uncovered. "You're even more beautiful than I'd imagined," he muttered hoarsely. "All dusky gold flesh and mauve tinted shadows."

The pad of his thumb pressed against a dark nipple, and he smiled as it rose to meet his ministrations. "You see?" he whispered. "Your body knows what it wants."

With a shudder she arched her back, her breasts full and hungering for more of his touch. When he cupped the underside of a silken globe and lifted it to his mouth, a tiny cry of fulfillment shattered the quiet as his teeth gently grazed her hardening nipple. "That's what I've waited to hear, Gypsy," he gasped, his clever tongue adding to her torment. "You wanting me, aching for my hands and my mouth, the way I ache for yours. Touch me, sweet thing. Let me feel your hands on my body."

Maria obeyed with dazed comprehension. As he dragged his open mouth slowly over the slope of her breast, she guided her hands down his chest until they circled his waist. As he paused to savor the taste of her smooth shoulder, she gripped the soft fabric of his knit sport shirt. His leather belt grazed her fingertips as she tugged the gold fabric free of his jeans. His tongue licked a maddening path across her collarbone, and she thrust her hands beneath the loosened material with an impatient murmur.

The heat of his skin spread warmth through her palms, up her arms and into her body. The blaze ignited all the cold, empty places inside of her, casting her mind adrift on a sea of fire. With a mewling cry of surrender she threw back her head, her throat arching to receive his moist, hungry kisses. His teeth bit against the pulse that acted as a throbbing barometer for her passion, then tenderly bathed the abrasion with his tongue. The moan she uttered vibrated against his lips, and he hurriedly lifted his head to capture the arousing sound with his mouth.

But he had miscalculated the extent of his arousal, and the softness of her yielding lips triggered the end of his control. The kiss became wild and devouring, his tongue dueling with hers for supremacy. With a guttural cry he drew back and jerked the end of her caftan free of her legs, clutching at her rounded thigh with fingers that didn't intend to mark her tender skin... but did.

She uttered a tiny gasp of protest, and he offered an apology in a voice almost too hoarse to be heard. He pressed a series of frantic kisses against her bruised flesh, each one punctuated by words of praise and abject appreciation. "You are... so sweet, so... beautiful. You make me... burn." His mouth guiding his hand, he caressed the inside of her thigh in search of a moister softness. "Let me... have you, Gypsy. Please don't push me away this time. Let me love you the way you were meant to be loved."

Nine

When his plea was met with silence, Drew's hands moved up until they engulfed Maria's slender waist. Grasping the edge of her lacy black panties with fingers that trembled, he slid them over her hips and down her long, exquisitely formed legs. Then he gently parted her knees and angled his body between the cradle of her thighs with the urgency of a man impatiently waiting on the edge of heaven.

He forgot to breathe as his eyes feasted on her lush beauty. With another moan he allowed the tips of his fingers to trace the smooth flare of her hips, while his thumbs sought the small indentation of her belly button. He heard the sharp gasp that exploded from her lungs, and his gaze rose until his eyes tangled with the ebony depths of her own. Her expression held a wealth of vulnerability and uncertainty, but there was also eager acceptance and shy reassurance in her eyes.

Suddenly he felt ready to burst with emotion, the excited acceleration of his heartbeat thrumming against the wall of his chest.

It was a moment out of time, one of mystery and anticipation he'd never experienced with any other woman. He was a supplicant at the gates of paradise, and humbled by the extent of his own Eve's trusting generosity. For the first time, Maria was holding nothing back. She was telling him without words that she was no longer running from him but toward him. The eyes that looked back at him held a sheen of moisture that caused the ache in his chest to constrict almost painfully, and he knew he wanted to give her the moon and stars and all he knew of earthly pleasures.

His body shuddered violently as his voraciously seeking mouth zeroed in on the place he was crazy to taste, and Maria's thoughts whirled within a barrage of sensation. There was warmth and slickness and jolting jabs of electricity triggering her body's response, and she suddenly understood the message she'd received from those intense, silver eyes so full of promise. With a small cry of surrender she stiffened, and her hips arched instinctively toward the source of her delight. The moan she uttered ended with a name, her vague plea one of both encouragement and shocked hesitancy.

"It's all right," a gruffly aroused voice soothed. "I've longed for the taste of your passion, love. Give yourself to me, and let me satisfy my hunger."

Maria had no choice. Her own need for satisfaction was thrusting her into a realm of intoxication she'd never known existed. Her chest rose and fell as she struggled to imbibe enough oxygen to survive this miracle of sensation, and every nerve ending in her body cried out for release. She writhed and twisted against his hungry mouth, completely out of control. A liquid burning poured through her, finally pooling into her belly with the engorged heat of flowing lava.

A new world was opening up to her, a world that both frightened and enticed. But as Drew's mouth and hands brought her to a bold, shocking level of self-awareness, she wondered if she would ever again experience true peace of mind. How long could she hide from the truth of what he was making her feel? How much of herself would go with him when they parted? She would certainly never forget his touch, which was burning an indelible memory into her brain. She had never known any experience could be so physically and emotionally shattering, or so terribly, wonderfully right.

Drew's lovemaking was reaching out and encompassing every atom of her being, and she was striving to absorb his very essence into her body. She was losing herself and becoming a part of him, and the realization was terrifying. Yet she couldn't resist; nor could she prevent the mewling sounds of pleasure that issued from her mouth. Her flesh was a writhing mass of jangling nerve ends, her mind nearly exploding with the wonder of what was happening to her.

She was reaching toward the sun, nirvana only a moment away. Then she was there, catapulted instantly through misty clouds and endless space. Colored lights burst behind her closed eyelids as she soared, until finally her journey ended in a devastating fire burst of sensation. A quavering cry of fulfillment burst from her throat and was answered by a deeply shaken, masculine groan that ended on a note of triumph.

Drew pressed kisses and muffled words of praise against the soft flesh of her belly, his deep, panting breath hot against her flesh. "You are a miracle," he whispered on a ragged inhalation. "My dreams of you were far less than the reality, and you are far more than I deserve, my Gypsy."

Carefully he rose to his feet, bending to lift her limp body into his arms. A fire still smoldered in the eyes that met hers, banked and yet ready to burst into a conflagration at any moment. "Which bedroom is yours?" he inquired gruffly.

He carried her toward the hallway as he spoke, his marauding mouth preventing her from forming a coherent reply. His teeth nipped at the swollen fullness of her bottom lip, and she responded to the teasing foray with a sated smile of bemusement. "Don't you dare fall asleep," he demanded, his accompanying laughter vibrating through her as her lips parted on a yawn. "In case you haven't noticed, I'm not quite finished yet, woman."

Although she responded to his warning tones with a giggle, she couldn't seem to hold her eyes open. "So sleepy," she murmured, her head finding a resting place against his shoulder.

Drew stopped dead center in the hallway, a mischievous grin indenting the edges of his mouth. Bending his head, he gave her kiss-swollen bottom lip another nip with his strong white teeth. This time the bite was sharp enough to regain her full attention, and she scowled up at him reprovingly. When his tongue bathed the tiny abrasions with comforting moisture, her frown disappeared as she automatically opened herself to the slow exploration of his tongue.

Maria's lips wanted to cling and to go on clinging, to press harder into his kiss until she didn't know where he ended and she began. She wanted more than he was giving her, but she was too shy to make any demands of her own. In an excess of frustration her fingers curled, her sharp nails digging into his neck. Drew's groan was a paean of arousal instead of pain, but the telling sound was enough to shock Maria from her absorption.

With a gasp she tore her greedy mouth from his, her eyes wide with bewilderment at the aggressiveness of her behavior. It was as though she were suddenly two people, one she knew and the other a total stranger. One hesitant and restrained, the other wild and uninhibited. One adapted to self-control, the other gloriously, vibrantly uncontrollable.

Suddenly ashamed, she lowered her eyes to the pulse throbbing at the base of Drew's throat, the faintness of her voice barely penetrating the raspiness of their combined breathing. "I'm sorry. I didn't mean to hurt you."

"You only hurt me when you stopped kissing me like a wild woman," he replied with a stilted laugh. "Pleasure and pain are sometimes indistinguishable, Gypsy. I almost went through the ceiling when you dug those sharp little nails into me."

"Don't," she mumbled, the color in her cheeks darkening with every second that passed. "I don't know what made me act that way. I'm not usually so...forward."

"You mean you're not usually so responsive," he corrected gently. "There should be no shame in mutual desire, Maria. Haven't you ever allowed feeling to take over and just let yourself go?''

"No," she whispered weakly. "In fact, I've never—"

"Then it's time you did," he interrupted, his voice husky with tension. "Lovemaking should be a feast of the senses, not an exercise in restraint. It's not a dance with all the moves planned in advance.

"Take what you want from me," he continued in an encouraging whisper, his eyes glittering with barely restrained excitement. "Satisfy your curiosity, and let me satisfy mine."

Held high against his broad chest, their lips were on a level. Maria slowly inclined her head, her breath trapped in her lungs as she tentatively pressed her mouth against Drew's. As though the initial contact burned, she hurriedly withdrew only to be drawn again toward the source of heat. This time she pressed harder, a slight frown of dissatisfaction appearing between her dark brows when his mouth failed to open. With a murmur of frustration her own lips parted, and the tip of her tongue peeked out to trace his warm flesh.

His patience at an end, his lips widened to encourage the eager entry of her tongue into his mouth. As it slipped inside and began to duel with his own, he uttered a harshly expressive moan. His knees grew weak as his passion increased into a flood surging through his bloodstream like a tidal wave, and his arms tightened around his precious burden as he leaned against the wall nearest him.

Maria greeted the resurgence of desire with stunned comprehension and eager curiosity. She was no longer content to react to Drew's lovemaking with ladylike restraint, and she began to touch him with avid hands as her tongue explored the sweet depths of his mouth. With a sigh she ended the kiss and watched in disbelief at her boldness as her hand plunged through the opening in his shirt. She heard a faintly uttered cry and realized the passionate whimper had come from her own throat.

Drew's pupils dilated as that betraying sound exploded in his brain, the dark centers expanding until they nearly obliterated the gray. "Go ahead and do it," he muttered through gritted teeth. "Heaven knows I want to feel your hands on me."

Maria didn't need his encouragement, since her trembling fingers were already tracing a path across his breastbone. She watched as they responded to a hidden message from her brain, which was filling her with the overwhelming need to touch him. Only then did she fully realize how right he'd been about her curiosity. She ached to imprint him on her senses...to feel the beat of his heart increase as she cupped his masculine nipple with her palm, to taste the salty tang of his flesh with her lips, to absorb his musky scent, to see his features tauten with passion as she satisfied her needs.

Without conscious volition her fingertips formed an arching curve and began to plunge and winnow through the curly mat of dark gold body hair covering Drew's broad chest. He groaned when her nails scraped across his flesh, and she shuddered violently in response. The helpless sound that erupted from the tense muscles of her throat came as a surprise, and she pressed her face against his shoulder as he uttered a pleased laugh.

Drew didn't try to battle her for supremacy, but instead encouraged her to explore her passion in her own time and in her own way. Although she kept her face hidden from him, slim fingers rose to tangle in his hair. She angled her head, her hands locking him in a vise as her mouth opened against the pulsing warmth of his throat. High, rounded breasts pushed against his chest, until two vibrantly beating hearts seemed to echo as one. Primitive instincts rose to urge him to complete their union where he stood, until holding himself in check became an agony.

Only he didn't want his first time with Maria to occur on a hallway carpet. He wanted her to remember their lovemaking as a romantic experience, not an animal coupling with no sensitivity and little finesse. She was aroused enough not to mind, and his own self-control was hanging by a thread. But now was not the time to lose it, and as he reminded himself of this his mouth firmed with resolution. If restraint cost him a measure of sanity, then so be it. He was going to give Maria his best or die trying.

Ten

Wrapping her arms more firmly around Drew's neck as he once again began to carry her down the hallway, Maria wondered if a woman had ever held such perfection in her arms. He was all hard muscle and warm sensuality, and the strength in his body no longer posed a threat to her existence. Instead, his entire being had become her haven of security, a place of caring and nurturing. She felt cherished in a way she had always longed to be, and needed with a depth of passion she hadn't thought anyone would ever feel for her.

With shyly awkward hesitancy she pressed another kiss against the pulse beating in the hollow of his throat, and her trembling increased as she savored the evidence of his life force with the tip of her tongue. A new urgency seemed to radiate from him at her touch, his stride lengthening as he entered her bedroom and lowered her feet to the floor.

With exquisite care he lifted her sole remaining garment over her head, leaving her naked and exposed to his molten gaze. Shyness still dictating her movements, Maria tried to shield herself with her arms in a classic pose of feminine modesty. But Drew refused to acknowledge her reticence and gently grasped her wrists until her arms were lowered to her sides. Meeting the obsidian mystery of her glistening eyes, he whispered, "You are glorious, the most beautiful woman I've ever seen. Please... don't hide yourself from me, Maria."

His hands slid up her arms to her shoulders as he urged her against his body with gentle yet firm insistence. His fingers lightly caressed her chin, sliding beneath the rounded curve as he tilted her face up for his inspection. For a long, poignant moment he studied her mouth, his expression curiously somber as he slowly negated the distance between them. Their lips met in a kiss sweeter than any that had gone before, a kiss that held a promise of eternity. His other hand burrowed beneath the hair at her neck, his palm sliding down the curve of her back to her waist.

By the time the kiss ended, Maria needed the support of that strong, encircling arm to keep herself from slumping to the floor. Her legs were shaking so badly she doubted if they would hold her weight much longer, and her own hands were wrapped around his biceps in a death grip. As he quickly leaned sideways to pull back the cream-and-rose comforter from her bed, the understanding grin he gave her was more of a grimace.

Top sheet and blanket received the same treatment. His movements were uncharacteristically jerky, his impatience obvious as he thrust the bedding against the rounded curve of the white wicker footboard. Yet when he turned to her once more, he used great care as he lifted her until she was reclining against the floral-patterned sheets. Maria sighed as the cool material soothed her heated flesh, and her eyes followed his every movement as he began to undress.

Drew fascinated and beguiled her. As he stripped off his shirt with hands that shook visibly, she gazed at the magnificence of his naked chest in near reverence. Each movement he made was poetry in motion. His superbly conditioned frame was sleek and mobile, the rippling play of muscles beneath his taut, sleek flesh capturing her intrigued gaze. He's the beautiful one, she mused, silently paying homage to the masculine grace and power of his body.

The downy spread of golden hair covering his firmly rounded pectorals narrowed into a thin, downward pointing line until it disappeared beneath the waistband of his snug, low-slung jeans. Her attention was fixed for long moments on his hands, which were unfastening the buckle of his belt. They were strong and confident, she realized with a shiver of anticipation, like the man himself. Then with a final tug and a frustrated mutter the metal buckle clicked open, and the full extent of his arousal became obvious.

Maria forgot to breathe, eyeing the straining bulge demanding to be released from its confinement in utter fascination. His tennis shoes were kicked off and his socks as quickly dispensed with, and then, jeans and briefs were shoved down his long, muscular legs. When Drew straightened, apparently unconcerned with his nudity, it was all she could do to stifle a gasp of trepidation. She certainly wasn't able to pretend nonchalance with the powerful evidence of his swollen manhood so vividly on display, any more than she could begin to hide the sudden uncertainty the sight of him aroused.

As he lowered himself beside her, Drew took one look at her face and smiled reassuringly. "Don't worry, love. I'm a big man and you're just a little slip of a female, but I'll take the greatest care with you."

"Drew, I think you should know..."

"Shh," he murmured against the fluttering pulse in her neck. "Just relax and let nature take its course. I promise I won't hurt you."

He wouldn't be able to help hurting her, but all at once it didn't matter. Nothing mattered but the warm mouth that began suckling at her breast, drawing on the hard, tight bud of her nipple until she moaned her pleasure aloud. Equal attention was paid to its twin, his head languidly roaming from side to side as she arched her back to facilitate his marauding mouth. A whimpering plea erupted from her parted lips, and she eagerly spread her open hands over his chest.

Her palms absorbed the rapid beat of his heart, which so closely matched the erratic rhythm of her own. The need to discover all the textures of his body overwhelmed her, and she eagerly ran her fingers through the hair on his chest. She marveled at its soft, cushiony texture against her hands. He muttered unintelligibly when her nails raked across his flesh, and she trembled in response. A keening cry erupted from the tense muscles of her throat, and with blind instinct she sought the small bud of one masculine nipple with the tip of her tongue. She was being carried away, desire firing her body with an instinctive sensuality she barely understood.

The primitive force of her emotions shocked her into withdrawing slightly, but Drew was beyond the point of noticing her momentary hesitation. With an intensity that wiped every other thought from her mind, he kissed and nibbled and licked at her lips until she was once again caught up in the magic he exuded. As she strained to draw in her next breath, his heated, mobile mouth slid down her arched throat, where he treated her round, firm breasts with the same intense absorbtion he'd bestowed on her lips.

She found herself arching mindlessly to meet the press of his tongue and scraping teeth against her pebble-hard nipples, while her hands clasped his head in a possessive demand for more of the same. By the time he parted her thighs to receive him, she was in a delirious state that completely obliterated any apprehension she might have felt.

As she accepted his heavy frame within the cradle of her thighs, he braced his weight on his elbows and stretched out over her body. His hands brushed aside the moist hair at her temples and cheeks, and as he began to sheathe himself inside of her he left a trail of greedy, tempestuous kisses against her mouth and forehead and pert, rounded chin.

Then with a powerful thrust of his hips he sought to complete their union, and froze when she cried out in unmistakable anguish. "Maria?" he gasped in bewilderment, his hands holding her face still when she would have averted her head from his discerning gaze.

He searched her eyes in shocked realization, and the lingering pain he saw reflected there caused him to utter a succinct curse. "I didn't know. Why in hell didn't you tell me?"

"It doesn't matter," she whispered faintly.

He shook his head, his features reflecting both self-disgust and guilt. "When I think of the things I've accused you of—the lovers my imagination has conjured up over the years through sheer jealousy..."

Maria pressed her fingers against his lips, a gentle light in her eyes. "Nothing matters now but this."

She lent emphasis to her words by giving a slight wriggle to her hips, her satisfaction obvious as he cried out in pleasure. With stubborn persistence he gritted his teeth as he tried to pull back, but he had gone too far too fast. When a rippling shiver convulsed his body, he closed his eyes as he accepted his human weakness. "I'm sorry," he muttered brokenly as he rested his sweat-moistened forehead against the scented hollow between her shoulder and neck. "I can't stop. I can't...."

With an instinct that began at the dawn of creation, Maria gripped him with her thighs and felt her woman's body stretch and widen to receive him fully. Her hands began to wander over the smooth, knotted musculature of his back, and with a soothing murmur she gently pressed her pelvis against him in unspoken encouragement. When no pain resulted from the movement, tentativeness gave way to an enthusiasm that soon had Drew moaning helplessly in her arms.

"Witch," he gasped, regaining his self-control by inches. Levering himself upward on shaking arms, he grinned down at her. "You nearly unmanned me there for a minute, but I've got your measure now."

Feeling every inch a sensual female and reveling in the metamorphosis, she retorted smugly, "You only think you do."

With maddening slowness he began to thrust and withdraw, a pleased, husky laugh erupting from his throat as he saw her eyes widen with amazement and then glaze over with passion. As her fingers dug into his back, he pressed his lips to one dainty ear and growled, "You were saying?"

"Drew," she whispered, her head beginning to toss from side to side on the lace-edged, floral-patterned pillowcase. "I didn't know it would feel like this. Oh, Drew!"

Her own hips began to follow the seductive cadence of his, and her back stiffened at the pleasure he was creating inside of her. With a sobbing moan her arms dropped to her sides, and she clutched at the rumpled sheets until her fingers ached. Her breasts rose and fell with each strained breath she drew into her lungs, their distended, roseate tips glistening from the moisture left behind by his suckling mouth.

Then the world exploded as Maria was blown apart by passion's fury, and she didn't know whether the scream echoing in her ears came from herself or the man she clung to so tightly. For long, exquisitely blissful moments she floated in space, all the colors of the rainbow spinning behind her lowered eyelids. A soft sigh of satisfaction issued from her parted lips, and as Drew lifted himself to lie beside her, she snuggled against him with a confidence born of the tenderness he'd shown her.

"Are you all right?"

The worry in his gravelly voice caused her to smile and press a reassuring kiss against his collarbone. "I'm wonderful," she whispered happily.

"That you are." His arms tightened around her, loosening slightly to allow him to slide a caressing hand down the long, tangled strands of hair spread across his chest. "Maria?"

"Mmm?" she murmured drowsily.

"Any regrets?"

For a brief moment the shadows of yesterday returned to haunt her, but she quickly pushed them away. She didn't want to think of all the reasons she shouldn't be here, wrapped in Drew's gentle arms. She would remain his lover for as long as fate allowed, and when they parted she would have memories of these stolen hours to sustain her.

Squirming to find an even more comfortable position against his warm body, she finally managed to give him the reassurance he sought with a negative shake of her head. But his question triggered her own uncertainties, and after several increasingly tense moments, she asked hesitantly, "Are you sorry, Drew?"

Placing a kiss against the crown of her head, he uttered a shaken laugh and moved with a suddenness that caused her to utter a startled gasp. There was a renewed flicker of passion in his eyes as he bent over her, and pure demand in the mouth that captured her own. "Do I seem remorseful?" he murmured against her tingling lips.

Her sleepiness dispersed like magic, and a slow, seductive smile curved her mouth. "I don't think so," she responded teasingly, "but I can't be sure. Why don't you provide me with a little more evidence, Counselor?"

"With pleasure, Gypsy."

Eleven

Drew yawned widely and shoved the filter on the coffee maker into place. Depressing the On button, he moved toward the sliding glass doors leading out onto Maria's minuscule back deck. Dressed only in the unbelted jeans he'd worn the night before, he twisted the metal bolt lock and slid open the door. His bare feet registered the pleasant feel of sun-warmed wood as he stepped onto the rectangular platform, and a small smile tugged at his mouth as he crossed the smoothly weathered boards.

A strong breeze wafted the scent of pine and resin against his face, and he inhaled with eager appreciation. Resting both hands against the wide surface of the wooden guardrail surrounding the deck, he listened to a couple of blue jays vociferously arguing squatting rights in a nearby oak. Otherwise he heard only the rustle of the wind through the trees and marveled at this bit of Eden tucked away in the center of a busy, frenetically paced city.

If he hadn't known better, he realized, he would have sworn he was in a chalet deep in some isolated forest glade. The noise of the busy streets nearby was muffled, the peacefulness of these surroundings protected by nature's amazingly effective leafy green sound wall. As he leaned his weight on his arms and glanced down at the manzanita-tangled, dew-dampened bracken below, he found himself wondering what miracle of oversight had kept this place from being swallowed up in the name of progress.

A movement to his left caught his attention, and he became interested in the antics of a sparrow nearly hidden by a wheat-colored clump of weeds. It was industriously poking a sharp beak into the dark, moist earth in search of breakfast, and Drew's grin widened as he murmured, "Don't you know it's the early bird that catches the worms, buddy?"

Although his feathered friend had gotten a late start this morning, Drew found himself envying the quick, energetic actions of the small brown bird. Personally he was teetering on the edge of exhaustion, which was a sad commentary for a man not yet considered middle-aged to have to admit. But fortunately for his self-esteem, he felt far from decrepit as he recalled the reason for his tiredness. Decrepit, hell, he thought exultantly, straightening to rub a hand lazily over his hair-roughened chest. Remembering other, smaller hands that had repeatedly followed the same path, he felt reborn!

He had done little more than catnap in between bouts of lovemaking last night, and by the time dawn had splattered the bedroom with light, his fate had been sealed. Glancing at the face next to his on the pillow, he'd wondered how he could have been so blind for so many years. Watching Maria sleep had made him experience a tenderness so strong and all-encompassing he'd been shocked into instant realization. It was then he had known, beyond a shadow of a doubt, that he would never again be content living on the fringes of her life.

Now, as he recalled the first time they'd made love, and that exquisite instant of becoming not two bodies but one, he finally understood the meaning of the word *commitment*. He also knew that his feelings toward Maria were a lifetime proposition, something he hadn't been certain of when he'd first asked her to marry him. Somewhere along the line she'd become an integral part of his very existence, he reasoned poignantly, the other half of his soul.

Straightening to raise his arms high over his head, he gave in to another yawn and stretched the final kinks out of his body. Realizing that a good dose of caffeine would dispel the last of his sleepiness, he turned and made his way back into the kitchen. Searching the overhead cabinet, he found one of the man-size mugs, which fit his far from dainty hand better than the delicate china cups Maria favored. Filling it to the brim with the strong, aromatic beverage, he took a fortifying sip before heading back outside.

He had reached the sliding glass door and was stepping through the opening, when the sound of the doorbell stopped him in his tracks. With a muttered imprecation, he hurried to answer the summons before it awakened Maria. Flicking open the lock with one hand while he cradled his mug in the other, he threw open the heavy wooden panel without once considering his state of undress. His sister and Charlie stood gaping at him from the hallway, both wearing identical expressions of shock.

"Uh-oh," he muttered sheepishly, a dull flush coloring his cheekbones. Gesturing them inside before the whole complex got a glimpse of him, he closed the door and lifted his mug in the air. "Coffee, anyone?"

A delighted smile had replaced the shock on Tricia's features, but Charlie was another matter entirely. His naturally ruddy complexion had paled considerably, and there was a distinctively angry gleam in his baby blues. There was also more than a hint of disillusion, which made Drew realize how much he had come to value the boy's good opinion.

"It's not what you're thinking," he stated abruptly, his gaze unwavering on Charlie's disapproving features. "I love her, dammit!"

"I knew it!" Tricia squealed, rushing forward and throwing her arms around her brother's waist. "I knew there was more than antagonism between the two of you, no matter how many times you guys went for each other's jugulars. When's the wedding?"

Barely managing to keep the rest of the liquid from slopping over the sides of his mug and onto the shiny tile floor of the entry, Drew held one arm aloft while circling his sister's narrow waist with the other. The corner of his mouth quirking betrayingly, he admitted, "We haven't gotten around to discussing the details yet."

Charlie squared his shoulders, his voice deceptively mild as he asked, "But you intend to, right?"

Drew couldn't take exception to the boy's attitude, knowing his protectiveness was based on his own affection for Maria. Releasing Tricia, he shifted his mug into his left hand and held out his right in Charlie's direction. "I'm going to get that woman of mine to the altar as soon as possible," he admitted in a voice rife with sincerity.

Finally a grin replaced Charlie's scowl, and he shook Drew's hand with enthusiasm. "All right!"

Tricia became dreamy eyed. "As your only sister and Maria's best friend I can be your matron of honor and Lynette could be the maid of honor and Charlie could..."

Drew's scowl was belied by twinkling eyes. "We're going to have a wedding, not a full-scale stage production."

Tricia didn't pay him the slightest attention, lost in her reverie. Charlie took advantage of the momentary silence with alacrity. "It sure took you long enough to stake your claim," he teased. "You've been dogging Maria's heels for quite a while now."

Drew's lips twisted, but there was a distinctly good-humored gleam lighting his gray eyes as he nodded. "Just like a tame puppy."

As though of one accord, the three of them crossed the living room and entered the sunny white-and-gold kitchen. With the ease of familiarity both Tricia and Charlie poured their own coffee and hurriedly joined Drew at the table. He glanced at his sister and his lips twisted ruefully. "I'd go and put my shirt on, but I don't want to wake Maria. She needs to rest."

A knowing smile greeted his words, twin dimples popping out on either side of Tricia's mouth. "I'll just bet she does."

Lifting his eyes toward heaven for guidance, Drew muttered, "Now stop that! You know how many extra hours she's been putting in at FACES headquarters lately. If she doesn't ease up, she's going to make herself sick."

A worried frown replaced Tricia's smile, and both she and Charlie nodded in agreement. "You won't get her to slow down with winter coming on," Charlie said.

"No, you won't," Tricia agreed. "Not until we've been able to find shelters for all the people still squatting down in the hollow beside the creek."

Drew's brows rose incredulously. "You mean there really is a creek around here?"

"Sure there is." Some of the animation left Charlie's face as he spoke, and he seemed to somehow distance himself as he continued with an explanation. "It's located below this apartment complex, but is far enough away from the main traffic areas to provide a natural hiding place for some of the homeless population."

He lowered his gaze to his coffee mug, his lips twisting with suppressed bitterness. "Most of Hayward's citizens have forgotten its existence, mainly because it's circled by private property and can only be reached by foot. The authorities haven't forgotten, but generally choose to turn a blind eye. I guess they figure that since the dirt is already under the rug and can't be seen, they have better things to do with their time. Other than staging a cleanup campaign to remove undesirables every now and then, the cops leave everyone pretty much alone."

Taking note of the harsh inflection in Charlie's voice, Drew said, "You sound as though you're speaking from firsthand experience."

"Hidden Creek was a way for Lynette and me to stay off the streets and out of sight. A cardboard shelter didn't provide much protection from the weather, or from some of the scum who would as soon kill you as look at you, but I couldn't take the chance of being arrested for loitering. The authorities would have taken my sister away, and probably put me in juvenile hall. So I carried a knife, and I never let Lynette out of my sight.''

When the boy's head rose in unspoken defiance, Drew was shocked by the look in his eyes. This was a Charlie he'd never seen before, one filled with hostility and anger and pain. There was violence there, too, a rage born of hopelessness and fear. This was the man-child Maria had taken into her home without consideration for her own safety, and he shivered inwardly as he thought of what might have happened if her belief in Charlie's intrinsic goodness had been unfounded.

Drew cleared his throat of the remnants of fear tightening his vocal cords and loosened the fingers that had formed a death grip around the heavy mug in his hand. As he inhaled its contents, the once-pleasing aroma made him feel sick. Forcing himself to relax, he leaned back against his chair and waited for Charlie to continue.

Visibly shaking his head to free himself of a past he wanted only to forget, Charlie complied with a lighter note in his voice. ''When the rains started, I had to get my sister out of there. She was sick and feverish, so I broke into one of Maria's empty apartments. I made Lynette lock herself inside while I went scrounging for food, but someone heard her coughing and reported the break-in. When I got back, Maria was there caring for Lynette, and eventually she convinced me she wouldn't turn us in to the authorities if we went home with her.

''Not that she had to do much convincing,'' Charlie added with a sheepish grin. ''The heat had been shut off after the previous tenants left, and it was darned cold in there.''

"That crazy woman!" Drew exploded, his eyes flashing fire at the potential danger to which Maria had exposed herself. "No offense, Charlie, but she's too damn trusting for her own good. She needs a keeper, that's for sure!"

Charlie's grin widened further. "Are you applying for the job?"

"Hell, no, I'm just taking it," Drew informed him imperiously, chuckling deeply when Charlie laughed in approval. "You know as well as I do that Maria would never get off her feminist high horse long enough to let me try my hand as her protector."

"You or any other male," Tricia retorted, indignant at the sexist direction the conversation had taken.

"You've got that right!"

The disgruntled exclamation came from the living room, and the three people seated around the table looked at each other in consternation. When Maria rounded the corner and passed through the archway into the kitchen, both Tricia and Charlie averted their eyes guiltily.

Drew, however, was made of sterner stuff. Ignoring his black-haired gypsy's disapproving glare, his gaze traveled with leisurely thoroughness over her delightfully rumpled, if militant, figure. "Good morning, babe," he greeted huskily. "Did you sleep well?"

Twelve

Maria's stance remained rigid with disapproval, but her continued silence failed to have any effect on Drew. She was wearing a blue robe old enough to have belonged to Methuselah, and just looking at her in that ratty, threadbare garment made him long to drag her back into the bedroom. Especially when he remembered what was beneath it, he added with inward amusement.

But knowing her contrary nature as well as he did, she would more than likely scream bloody murder and force Charlie to come to her rescue. He had no objection to making her scream, he thought with a galloping heartbeat, but peeling her redheaded Galahad off the ceiling would require more effort than he felt capable of expending at the moment.

Deciding a little pampering was in order, he rose and casually gestured for her to take his chair. "Have a seat, and I'll get you a nice hot cup of coffee, sweet thing. That'll put a twinkle back in your lovely black eyes."

Maria was glaring a hole in Drew's back, but a giggle distracted her attention. Her head swiveled toward Tricia, who was sitting suspiciously still with a hand clamped over her mouth. "What are you laughing at?" she asked belligerently.

"Babe? Sweet thing?" Tricia chortled, her own eyes dancing at this unfamiliar glimpse of her brother as a devoted swain. "Oh, Lord, I can't stand it!"

Completely discarding her dignity, Tricia shoved her coffee cup out of the way and laid her blond head down on her crossed arms. Her shoulders were shaking betrayingly, while muffled choking sounds erupted from her mouth.

Muttering a few choice words of disgust, Maria plopped down in the chair Drew had pulled out for her without uttering another word. Her so-called friend wouldn't be worth diddly until she'd recovered from her bout of hysteria, and her own temper was giving her a terrific headache. This was the morning after the night before all right, she thought with gritted teeth, and the pounding inside her skull was entirely the fault of that blond imp of Satan eyeing her so fatuously. There wouldn't have been a night before if it hadn't been for him!

Becoming lovers should have remained a private matter between her and Drew, but there was certainly no hope of that now. If only he hadn't opened the door to Charlie and Tricia, especially with his clothes half-off! He certainly should have known better than to place her in this untenable situation. She just hadn't been prepared to have anyone know of the changes in their relationship, and especially not his own sister. That regrettable romantic streak of Tricia's might be well hidden beneath the mature, coolly sophisticated facade she'd adopted since her marriage, but Maria didn't doubt its continued existence. In fact, as soon as her friend stopped laughing she'd more than likely start badgering her to start shopping for a wedding dress.

At the thought, Maria quickly lowered her head to hide the tears that suddenly filled her eyes. Blinking rapidly, she tried not to envision a church filled with flowers, or herself walking toward Drew down a long, petal-strewn aisle. Those kinds of visions were suitable for other women to dream of... never for her. Dreams of orange blossoms and white lace had been the price she'd paid for survival, she thought bitterly, and it was much too late to wish it could be otherwise.

Rubbing her temples fretfully, she glanced across the table at Charlie. Her depressed mood wasn't improved when she noticed the look on his face. His mouth was compressed manfully, but his heightened complexion gave him away. It nearly matched the fiery cast of his hair, but a single threatening glance from her flashing eyes was enough to keep him from giving in to his amusement.

Drew strolled forward, gingerly carrying Maria's dainty cup and saucer in his large hand. Placing it down on the corner of the table nearest him, he grasped the back of her chair and bent down to whisper in her ear. "I'm going to go and finish dressing, honey."

Remembering having to tiptoe around the rest of his clothing when she'd gotten out of bed, she nodded

jerkily and almost cringed with embarrassment. But
darn it, this was her first morning after and she had
every right to be a little rattled! "Your shirt is still on
the floor," she whispered. "I was going to hang it up,
but I heard voices and..."

"I could have done that myself," he stated firmly.
"You're not my personal French maid. I could have
put the stupid thing on and saved you a great deal of
embarrassment."

He tilted her chin up with a curled index finger and
murmured teasingly, "But since we've been found out,
why not come with me now, Gypsy? I'll get rid of
Tricia and Charlie, and we can take a long, relaxing
shower together. If we hang my shirt up in the bathroom, I guarantee all the wrinkles will have disappeared by the time we're finished."

Just the thought caused a melting sensation to storm
her defenses, and she could vividly picture herself
sliding down the drain along with the bathwater. His
sensual rasp rippled over her skin and penetrated her
pores, and the promising gleam in his silver eyes would
have made her knees buckle if she'd been standing.

Maria's breath hissed inward, and she was ready to
make a grab for him until she remembered their au-
dience. Although he'd spoken too softly for the other
two to hear, she had to brace herself to steal a quick
glance in their direction. Relieved to discover her
friends caught up in their own conversation, Maria
glanced back toward Drew and edged away from his
caressing hand. "I prefer to bathe in private," she
blurted out.

She had intended to treat his suggestion with sophisticated hauteur and was dismayed by the primly
shocked tone in her voice. Her reddening cheeks and

horrified expression revived his laughter, which seemed to feather her skin in softly tickling waves. "Don't knock it until you've tried it, sweet thing," he whispered, one brow arching wickedly. "There's nothing like the feel of soap-slicked hands sliding over your skin, making you—"

With a gasp she clamped a hand over his smiling mouth. "Oh, hush!"

He tickled her palm with the tip of his tongue, his eyes dancing when she jerked it away. "Will you stop teasing me, you horrible man?"

"First you have to agree to come home with me," he informed her with mock sternness. "We can have a picnic lunch on the patio, and then spend the rest of the day soaking up the sun by the pool. And if you're extra nice to me, I might even take you somewhere special for dinner."

"That's blackmail," she retorted, trying not to smile. "You can take your special dinner and sh—" she began, but the warmth of his mouth against hers successfully halted her tirade. She had very little oxygen remaining in her lungs by the time he lifted his head, certainly not enough to consider telling him off.

"Here you go," he murmured, sliding her coffee across the table until it rested in front of her. "Be back in a second."

With a wave for their two smug-faced observers, he left and Maria latched onto her cup with the enthusiasm of a drowning woman scrabbling at a floating log. She kept her eyes trained on the leaf-patterned saucer, refusing to look up at her friends. The sound of the shower starting up only added to her lack of composure, seeming to emphasize the new intimacy between herself and Drew like an exclamation point at the end of a sentence.

Not that she needed reaffirmation. She no longer had to rely on fantasy to visualize him standing naked, his taut skin gleaming as the water cascaded off his soap-lathered body. Nor did she need to concentrate to remember the feel of that firmly muscled torso against her hands, or the enveloping warmth of his heavy frame as he pressed into her yielding flesh. Erotic flashbacks took form in her mind, coming one after the other in amazing detail. Squirming in her chair at the memories, she continued to moisten her drying mouth with reviving sips of the coffee she clasped between sweating palms.

For heaven's sake, get a hold of yourself, Maria! The unspoken demand held an element of panic, she was quick to acknowledge. If she didn't start acting like a grown woman instead of a besotted child, Drew was going to realize just how much supremacy he'd gained over her with their lovemaking. She didn't want him to see evidence of the new, shattering vulnerability she'd discovered in herself upon waking this morning. She didn't want him to sense the inner turmoil that was tearing her to pieces inside.

As she took another mouthful of coffee and inhaled its familiar scent with closed eyelids, she thought frantically, I don't love him . . . I don't! All I'm feeling toward him is a residual carryover from the hours spent in his arms. It's just sex, that's all! Just sex? she countered weakly, a fluid heat running through her middle that had nothing to do with the beverage she'd just swallowed.

As she recalled the entirety of her response to Drew's touch, she knew a moment of despair. The vibrant, enthralled woman she saw in her mind's eye was based on a new and disturbingly physical knowledge of herself. All these years she had managed to repress her sensual nature, considering love too risky for someone like her. Then why had she lowered her defences and allowed Drew to pierce both her heart and her soul?

Flinching away from the question, Tricia's voice interrupted her reveries. "What's the matter, Maria? Did you burn your mouth?"

Her friend's concern made her smile and shake off her introspective mood. Without considering the interpretation that might be placed on her words, she said, "I'm fine. My lip is a little sensitive, that's all."

The other woman grinned knowingly. "I wonder why?"

Disconcerted, Maria quickly scanned the room in search of Drew, some of her embarrassment fading when she noticed he hadn't yet returned to the kitchen. Clearing her throat, she managed a faint but emotive warning. "Stop looking so smug, Patricia Ann, or I'll let Marc know you went to see those male strippers for your birthday last month."

"You were the one who took me," she protested loudly.

"I'm not married."

Tricia's face began to glow. "But you're going to be, and I couldn't be happier. At long last, the delay due, I might add, to the pigheadedness of the two people I love most in the world, we'll finally be sisters."

"I'm happy for you, too, Maria," Charlie added.

Although unbelievably touched by the unfeigned pleasure in her friends' voices, Maria flinched inwardly. As she had feared, Tricia had taken it for granted that she and Drew would be planning a wedding. And although she knew she should correct her mistaken assumption, she couldn't bear to see the joy fade from her face. God knows it had been too long since she'd seen so much enthusiasm in those gentle blue eyes, and Maria couldn't bring herself to disillusion her.

Searching her mind for a change of subject, after several minutes all she managed to utter was a trite inquiry. "By the way, what are you two doing here?"

Luckily for her, the question proved surprisingly effective. Her friends glanced at each other in consternation, their expressions twin examples of unvoiced conjecture. "Have you forgotten our plans for this afternoon?" Charlie asked, his voice tentative as he made allowances for Maria's forgetfulness.

She gasped in dismay as his words triggered her memory. "Oh, Lord, it's delivery day! How could it have slipped my mind?"

"At least you've got a good reason for forgetting." Tricia grinned irrepressibly. "We stopped off at Marge's first, and she came to the door in fuzzy pink slippers."

"Yeah," Charlie added with a laugh. "They had beady eyes, a black nose, and bunny ears that flopped up and down when she walked. I wonder if she can get me a pair for Lynette?"

Giving him a distracted smile, Maria hurriedly swallowed the last of her coffee. "How many recruits have you managed to round up, Charlie?"

"Half a dozen from work, and several of the men from FACES," he informed her with an air of satisfaction. "We won't have any trouble getting all of the heavier boxes of canned goods down the hill in one trip, and you women should be able to manage the clothing and blankets. The shipment of wood to build lean-tos hasn't arrived yet, so we'll have to schedule that delivery later in the month.''

He was rewarded with a vibrant grin and a thumbs-up sign from Maria. "That's great!" she exclaimed with renewed enthusiasm, pathetically grateful for the chance to put an end to this uncomfortable get-together. "Give me twenty minutes to shower and dress, and I'll meet you both in the storeroom."

Maria jumped to her feet and began to turn but ran face first into an unyielding object. It was Drew's chest, and his large hands cupped her shoulders before she could back away. In clipped tones, he asked, "Have I missed something?"

Maria pulled her bruised nose away from his recently donned, not too wrinkled shirt, her eyes evasive as she chirped brightly, "Not a thing."

His gaze narrowed on her guilty features. "Then why the hurry?"

Not waiting for her to reply, he lifted his eyes in Charlie's direction. "What's going on?"

Naturally responding to the authority in the older man's voice, Charlie hurriedly explained their plans to take some supplies they'd collected down to Hidden Creek.

"Charlie set up donation stations at work," Tricia interjected enthusiastically, "and I've made the rounds of all of my friends. Maria talked a couple of neighborhood churches into donating to the cause, and the response was even greater than we anticipated."

"So much for spending a restful day together," Drew muttered beneath his breath, with a darkling glance in Maria's direction.

Peeking up at him through her lashes, Maria managed to utter a simple apology. "I'm sorry about this, Drew. I don't usually forget anything this important."

"Then you didn't leave me out of your plans intentionally?"

Hearing the note of pained conjecture in his voice, she lifted shocked eyes to his face. "Of course not!"

As she sensed the escalating tension between her friend and her brother, Tricia shot Charlie a meaningful glance and pointed in the direction of the entryway. Charlie nodded and followed her from the room, but the other occupants of the kitchen were too preoccupied with each other to notice. "Why would you think such a thing, Drew?" Maria questioned gently.

"I haven't been fooling myself into thinking you were eager for my company these past few weeks, honey. Most of the time you've barely tolerated my presence."

Unable to completely deny the accusation, Maria shrugged uneasily. "I've grown used to being alone, and it's difficult to alter the habits of a lifetime. I'm sorry if I've been rude."

"Rudeness be damned," he burst out, releasing her and lowering his arms to his sides. "I've forced my way into your life, little one. Now I need to know if you really want me there."

Slowly she lifted her hands and placed them against his chest, her eyes never leaving his. "I can't give you any promises for the future," she whispered huskily, "but I want to be with you, Drew. Can we take it one day at a time for now?"

"One day at a time," he agreed softly.

* * *

The late September day was fading to a close as Maria circled the amusement park grounds for what seemed the hundredth time. Her feet ached from walking, her body felt bruised from some of the wilder rides, and her head ached from the noise around her. And to think she was the one who had talked Drew into taking Lynette and her best friend, Sarah, on this outing, she thought tiredly.

At the moment, her young blond friend was jumping up and down at her side with eagerness, her voice pleading. "Lynette, I am not getting on that thing again," Maria informed the bloodthirsty minx firmly. "I almost ended up with whiplash the first time. Make Drew go with you. He's a lot more stiff-necked than I am. The double-decker carousel is more my speed."

"The merry-go-round is for babies," Lynette taunted with a grin.

Maria shot her an indignant look. "Anyway, the park will be closing soon."

"Aw, it won't close until after they shoot off the fireworks, and that won't be till the sun goes down. We've got plenty of time."

A pair of slender arms snaked around Maria's neck, and she found herself having to look up to meet the teenager's winsome blue eyes. When had her little one gotten so tall? she wondered with a pang of awareness. Soon the child would completely give way to the emerging woman, and Lynette would be dragging a boyfriend around the amusement park instead of her aging, decrepit pal. The thought almost egged Maria into agreeing to another ride on the Demon... almost, but not quite.

"Please, Maria?"

Glancing over Lynette's shoulder, Maria listened to the loud rumble of the roller coaster and shuddered delicately. "No way, Jose!"

"Drew," Lynette wailed, turning a pouting mouth in the smiling man's direction. "Just one more ride before the park closes?"

Pointing toward petite, brown-haired Sarah, who was already standing in line for the Demon, he asked, "Why don't you want to ride with your friend?"

"Sarah's ridden hundreds of times," she informed him with nary a blink of her long lashes at the exaggeration. "She doesn't mind going on by herself, and I'd rather go with Maria."

Although flattered, Maria eyed her suspiciously. "Why?"

"Because you're a lot more fun." Lynette's grin widened with the typical impertinence of a thirteen-year-old secure in the affection of an adult. "That scream of yours is awesome!"

Warned by the expression in Maria's dark eyes, Lynette giggled and quickly jumped out of swatting range. With a wave of her hand she joined Sarah in line, and Maria glanced ruefully at Drew. "The little sadist!"

"And you love every minute you have with her. You're good with kids," he tacked on quietly. "You need to have a couple of your own."

But for Maria children meant marriage, and marriage meant potential disaster. This was not the first time Drew had mentioned children in relation to her, and she was afraid it wouldn't be the last. He left her with no doubt that he still wanted to marry her, but whenever the subject came up she did her best to divert his attention.

Since they'd become lovers, a new and unexpected intensity had entered their relationship, one that caused her to become tense and defensive whenever he alluded to a more permanent commitment between them. Knowing such a conversation would mark the beginning of the end, she had so far managed to avoid a serious discussion of the future.

She didn't know how much longer she could stave off the inevitable though, especially in view of Drew's increasing impatience. He had grown quiet and unnaturally somber of late, his usual teasing manner toward her conspicuously absent. Often she found him watching her with a curiously resigned sadness in his eyes, as if he sensed that the laughing, smiling face she presented to him was a sham.

But what he couldn't begin to realize was that no matter how hard she struggled to keep her inner self apart and inviolate, inside she was crying for all the tomorrows they would never share. As she was now, she thought, suppressed grief tightening her chest until she wanted to scream aloud in agony. Dear God, she wanted it all—the wedding ring, the babies, the years of growing old together.

How she ached to clutch at him like a frightened child, to cling to him until the specters of her past disappeared. This was what she had always feared, she realized, this unbearable longing for permanence in Drew's life. When he made love to her she felt herself slip into the very essence of his being, safe and protected from harm. She wanted to bask in his warmth and yield to his strength and demand all the forever promises she'd never been given in her life.

But they couldn't spend all their time making love. Inevitably the world would intrude, and some upwardly mobile reporter would uncover her secret. She could bear it if it wasn't for Drew. She had long ago learned to counter scorn and rejection with indifference, but she could never be indifferent to him.

Nor could she bear putting him in the position of having to choose between her and the respect he'd earned from his contemporaries. That the choice would eventually come about was inevitable, given his media visibility. She was certain he would reach and even exceed his goals in life, she thought sadly, if she wasn't there to hold him back.

With a shocking abruptness that caused her to jump in reaction, Drew's voice penetrated her self-absorption. "The girls are almost ready to board."

His quiet observation sounded stilted as he glanced in her direction, his own expression distracted as he studied her closed expression. "Why don't we head over and meet them at the exit gate?"

Although she forced a smile and nodded, she deliberately avoided meeting his eyes. With more concentration than the action merited, she watched Lynette and Sarah progress in the line. Finally the two girls reached the platform and rushed toward the linked line of cars, their long, coltish legs a blur of movement as they disappeared out of sight.

The sun was beginning to set, the sky reflecting a final glorious burst of color before succumbing to the black velvet night. As she and Drew strolled to where the girls would eventually disembark, she was glad of the dimness, which shielded her expression. Soon the fireworks display Lynette had mentioned would herald the park's closing. Lights would be turned off, and the shouts and laughter silenced. This special day would become just one more treasured memory of Drew to add to all of those already stored in her heart.

Drew could feel the familiar tension gripping his body as he approached the entrance to Maria's apartment complex. He could blame his uneasiness on the grueling day he'd just spent in court, or the sultry weather, which had aggravated his temper and bathed his body in perspiration. But neither work nor weather was at the root of his mental turmoil, he realized grimly.

He stared up at the double glass doors leading into the building, his emotions as unsteady as his nerves. A cloud of depression seemed to hang over him like a smothering curtain, and the glorious surge of anticipation that used to fire his blood on previous visits to Maria was missing. He struggled to subdue a growing sense of grievance, needing this moment to mourn his loss.

Dread certainty crept over him, a nebulous feeling that somehow or other he'd taken a wrong turn in his relationship with Maria, a misstep that would eventually place her beyond his reach. Her manner was becoming more distant, her smiles less frequent. She was slipping away from him, and he didn't know what in hell to do about it!

Glancing down at the keys in his hand, he remembered the night she'd given them to him. There had been an expression of shy hesitation on her face when she'd handed him the key ring with his personal initial embedded in the clasp, as though she weren't quite certain he would want her offering.

He had reassured her with a kiss that had left them both breathless and sent them hotfooted in the direction of the bedroom. The key ring had ended up forgotten on top of her dresser, while they had escaped into their own personal world of the senses. Could two people touch the edge of heaven without paying a price for the privilege? he wondered sadly.

Apparently not. Making love to his beautiful gypsy was a little like riding one of the roller coasters she was so frightened of, he decided with a bitterly unamused smile. There were incredible, soaring highs that wrenched his body apart and sent his mind spinning, and lows that occurred so suddenly he was never prepared for the downward spiral. When he allowed rationality to affect his judgment, he wondered if the woman he loved was wise to be afraid.

Drew fitted the key into the lock and pushed the heavy door open with restrained violence. As it swung closed behind him, he heard the click as the automatic locking device once again slipped into place. He felt trapped suddenly and gritted his teeth at the sensation. His footsteps echoed hollowly in the tiled entry foyer, the disembodied sound marking his progress toward the hallway. Once there he was relieved to have his tread muffled by the thick carpeting, until the walls themselves seemed to close in on him.

He shouldn't have come here tonight, he thought with a rising sense of panic. His mood was too explosive, his temper too uncertain, and his patience nonexistent. He felt poised on a cliff edge, ready to jump and not too concerned with whether or not he hit bottom. It was then, as he stood staring blindly at Maria's door, that a sudden realization struck him with the force of a blow to the stomach.

As he searched out the second key on the ring she'd given him and fitted it into her door, he knew that tonight he was going to go for broke and once again ask Maria to marry him. And this time, he vowed silently, she was going to take him seriously. He had done as she wanted and taken their relationship one day at a time, but now it was time to collect on those promises for the future she had thus far avoided giving him.

Drew could always sense when Maria was close, and he knew the apartment was empty the minute he crossed the threshold. Closing the door behind him, he frowned at the single lamp burning in the living room, which was always left on when she went anywhere. From force of habit he automatically reached out to switch on the light in the entry hall, subconsciously relieved when the shadows surrounding him were dispersed.

When he'd spoken to her this afternoon, it had been to let her know he wouldn't be coming by tonight. She'd seemed vaguely relieved, which hadn't uplifted his spirits any, but she hadn't mentioned any plans for this evening. But then why would she? he asked himself bitterly. On more occasions than he wanted to remember, she'd decried his increasing possessiveness and made it clear that he had no right to question her movements.

She would cling to that damned independence of hers with her last ounce of determination, he thought angrily, but that didn't prevent him from worrying about her. This complex was heavily wooded, with too many places for an assailant to hide and await a victim, especially after dark. He'd thrown a fit upon discovering her habit of visiting Hidden Creek on her own, without the least regard for her safety. Although she'd promised not to do so again, a sudden suspicion sent him rushing to the phone.

He tried Charlie's number first, but when he got no response he dialed Marge. She answered with a breathy greeting, as though she'd been laughing when she picked up the receiver. "Marge, this is Drew."

Before he could continue, she blurted, "You must be a mind reader, honey. I was just thinking of calling to invite you and Maria over for a game of Monopoly. Lynette's here, and I need a little adult support. She's beating the pants off me."

His heartbeat accelerated as his tension grew, leaving behind a sinking sensation in his chest. "Then Maria's not there?"

"Why, no, I haven't seen her since late afternoon."

He inhaled harshly, fighting to prevent his voice from reflecting his increasing panic. "She didn't mention any plans to go out tonight?"

"No, but that's not unusual," Marge stated. "You know Maria."

Yes, he thought gloomily, he knew Maria's stubbornly prideful streak better than anyone. Clearing his throat to loosen the tightness accumulating there, he asked, "Where's Charlie? Maybe he knows where she's gone."

"He's working overtime," Marge informed him, a note of concern entering her voice. "That's why Lynette's staying with me tonight."

Marge broke off what she was saying with a hasty, "Hold on a second, Drew. Lynette's trying to get my attention. Maybe she knows where Maria has gone."

While he waited, he heard a muffled conversation in the background, as though Marge had placed her hand over the receiver. He shifted from one foot to the other with growing impatience and rubbed his hand repeatedly over the knotting muscles forming in the back of his neck. Finally she came back on the line, but what she had to say was hardly reassuring.

"There's a family with a sick child waiting for room to become available in one of our shelters. They're camped by Hidden Creek," she informed him uneasily. "Maria took the mother and baby to the free clinic last week, but yesterday Lynette overheard Maria telling Charlie that she planned to check up on the little one."

Marge paused for a moment as a new thought occurred to her, and a note of relief entered her voice. "Have you checked with Tricia? I bet that's where she's gone."

"My sister is at her cabin in Pescadero," he informed her harshly. "She's not due back for another week."

"I'm sure Maria's all right, Drew," Marge stated with false cheer. "She wouldn't have been foolish enough to go down to the creek alone at this time of night."

"Wouldn't she?"

A poignant silence followed his question, and when Marge replied it was with worried hesitancy. "It might be a good idea if you went looking for her, just to be on the safe side."

"It might at that," he muttered, pausing long enough to utter a distracted goodbye before hanging up the phone.

Thirteen

The overgrown, weed-infested path down to Hidden Creek was steep and irregular, but Drew had no need of the high-powered flashlight he carried to see his way. The moon overhead was like a bright beacon illuminating the rocky soil whose parameters were clearly defined by the countless number of feet that had forged this trail over the years.

A hardy-rooted clump of manzanita had broken its boundary and encroached onto the path. Pausing before trying to navigate the reddish, twisted roots that could wreak havoc on an unwary ankle, he raised his head as the sound of voices penetrated his isolation. He stiffened as he recognized Maria's light, breathy trill of laughter, which was accompanied by a deeper, more masculine chuckle. Instantly his anger increased until he thought he would blow apart at the seams.

Maria was still laughing as she rounded the bend in the path, her fluid stride and ethereal loveliness causing the breath to catch in Drew's throat. She was wearing tightly fitted black jeans, black rope sandals, a silver medallion-patterned Navajo belt and a rose-colored blouse with a black embroidered pattern etched around the gathered, elasticized neckline. With her hair flowing loosely around her pale oval face, she was an enchanting contrast of light and dark, substance and fantasy, reality and dream.

But the individual who sauntered out of the woods at her side was no fantasy figure, and the sight of him did nothing to alleviate Drew's temper. He was a huge bear of a man with a massively muscled chest, thick neck, and legs as big around as tree trunks. He was dressed in a dark-checked wool Pendelton that was stretched over his large belly and hung to his hips. The waist-length black leather jacket he wore over the shirt had seen better days, as had its heavily jowled owner. Both showed signs of having been pushed to the limit of endurance in a hostile environment, and neither could lay claim to cleanliness.

"Drew," Maria called out in surprise as soon as she spotted him. "How did you know I'd be here?"

"Not from anything you said, that's for sure," he growled accusingly.

Maria's face became the picture of guilt. "Uh-oh! Am I in trouble?"

"Dammit, Maria, you promised me you wouldn't go to Hidden Creek on your own at night!"

"I know, but after you called I got restless," she explained ruefully. "Charlie was working tonight, and I wanted to check on the Henderson baby."

Realizing she was practically tripping over her own tongue in an effort to justify her actions, she suddenly thrust out her chin and eyed him with disfavor. "Anyway, I left before dark."

"It's now after nine-thirty," he drawled softly, "and in case you haven't noticed, the sun did its disappearing act a long time ago."

Her chin rose higher as she gestured to the man at her side. "That's why Bud insisted on walking me back. I've been perfectly safe, I assure you."

Drew studied her companion with marked insolence. "And I bet you haven't known your friend for more than two minutes."

"Eight years, actually," the subject of Drew's disapproval interjected, his gentle, husky voice a curious contrast to his appearance.

Oblivious to the interruption, Drew glared at Maria and uttered his next statement with cold precision. "I've told you before, you're too damn trusting!"

Crossing her arms in front of her, she stared at him with open defiance. "And just who elected you my guardian angel?"

"Someone has to keep you out of trouble, and God wouldn't be cruel enough to lay that thankless task on one of his deputies. You'd make an angel so nervous he'd start pulling feathers out of his wings."

A bellow of laughter interrupted their argument, and two heads jerked toward the sound in surprise. "Just what's so funny, Bud Engel?" Maria questioned with deceptive softness.

"Looks like you finally got ahold of a man who might be able to drum some sense into that pretty head of yours, honey." Two narrow-lidded dark eyes fixed themselves on Drew with an intensity that pierced him to the marrow. "Are you that Sinclair fella I've been hearing about?"

His expression startled, Drew nodded an affirmative. "Maria's mentioned me?"

"Nah, she's as closed as a clam about her private business," the older man derided with a hearty snort, "but word gets around. There are a lot of us who worry about this little gal."

Drew shot Maria a triumphant glance before turning back to his unexpected ally. "Us?" he questioned.

"A good many of the folks Maria has helped, and a few of us down at the station."

When Drew frowned in puzzlement, Bud said, "Don't let appearances fool you, son. I'm with the Hayward Police Department, and Tom Phelps was my partner before he retired. Taught this ol' Idaho farm boy near everything he knows about police work. Now that my wife's passed on I spend a bit of time as a FACES volunteer. Kind of off-duty undercover surveillance, if you like."

"Bud and a few of his friends from the department take turns camping at Hidden Creek during their off-duty hours," Maria praised warmly. This time it was her expression that clearly reflected triumph as she turned to Drew. "Most of the homeless are honest, hardworking people down on their luck, but there are exceptions. Bud and his fellow officers help keep the toughs and drug pushers in line.

"They also warn us when there's a sweep scheduled," she added with a distinct twinkle in the eyes she again turned toward her friend.

Drew frowned in confusion. "A sweep?"

"Yeah, although that's inside information and not to be blabbed about," Bud responded with a reproving glare aimed at Maria. "Periodically the city hotshots put pressure on the department. When that happens we're forced to make a sweep of the known unauthorized shelter areas, and round up the homeless. I give Maria time to clear this area and keep the Creek People out of jail. Hell, the poor devils need someone on their side, and they sure won't get much help from publicity-mad politicians."

"Bud doesn't like politicians," Maria remarked smugly.

"Now don't you go putting words in my mouth, Miss Priss!"

Bud shared a masculine look of understanding with Drew, which made Maria bristle, and she glared at each of them in turn. "I should have known you guys would end up soul mates," she muttered disparagingly. "Put two Neanderthals together, and you end up with a couple of male chauvinist pigs."

Not a bit put out by the insult, Drew grinned at the older man and held out his hand. "I'm pleased to have met you, Mr. Engel, but I think it's time I got Maria home. She gets mouthy when she's tired."

"The name's Bud, son." Gripping Drew's hand with enough enthusiasm to crush his bones, he added, "Don't pay her no mind when she smarts off, and she'll fall into line sooner or later."

"I'll do no such thing," Maria gasped indignantly. "Bud Engel, how dare you . . . ?"

She was still on the upswing of a temper tantrum when Drew gripped her arm and began dragging her back along the path. "You might as well put a lid on it, Gypsy. Your friend is already out of shouting range.''

Maria's mouth snapped closed, and the glare she aimed in his direction was murderous. Without another word, she jerked her arm out of his hold and stormed past him with little regard for her flimsy footwear. A sharp rock penetrated the sole of her sandal, and she winced as pain shot through her foot. She should have changed into a pair of sturdy shoes before leaving home, but her decision to visit Hidden Creek had been made on impulse. As so many of her decisions were made nowadays, she thought derisively.

Most of the time she was like a squirrel in a cage, leaping from one end to the other with compulsive mindlessness. Her relationship with Drew was causing changes in her personality, which dismayed and frightened her, so much so that she was becoming a stranger to herself. She felt as though her life had become a crazy kaleidoscope of emotions, spinning her around and around until she didn't know where or who she was any longer.

She wanted to get off the merry-go-round, but Drew kept it perpetually spinning. A descent would mean certain injury, and she couldn't bear the thought of the pain she would suffer without him by her side. Yet trying for the brass ring would be an exercise in futility. It was too far out of her reach, and even if she managed to claim the prize, she knew it would be knocked out of her hand eventually.

The snap of a twig sounded behind her, and with a choked cry she began to run. She couldn't justify her actions, any more than she could explain the sudden panic causing her heart to pound and her vision to cloud. She was running blind, veering off the path and becoming enveloped in the ominous gloom of the woods. Twisted branches seemed to reach out for her like nightmare hands, and her arms rose to protect herself from their clawing grasp.

A voice cried out behind her, its very familiarity only increasing her frantic flight. "For God's sake, stop!" Drew shouted. "Do you want to break your damn fool neck?"

All she wanted was to escape, from him, from herself, and from the torment of her thoughts. Her breath was bursting in and out of her lungs in sobbing gasps as she broke into a small clearing, and her legs were leaden weights that gave out on her with a suddenness that sent her tumbling to the bracken-covered ground. She lay stunned and unresponsive for a blessedly quiet moment, but soon thundering footsteps heralded Drew's arrival.

"Are you crazy?" he questioned harshly, his breath as irregular as her own. "What in hell came over you?"

He dropped to his knees beside her, and she instinctively put out her hand to fend him off. Moonlight streamed through the leafy canopy overhead and reflected off her silver bangle bracelet watch. The medallions hanging from her ears and from the delicate chain around her neck matched the belt circling her slim waist, and she wondered if she preferred silver jewelry because it was the color of Drew's eyes.

Slowly she spread open her fingers and felt his heat through the thinness of his white long-sleeved dress shirt. He had removed his tie, and the top three buttons were unfastened. Her tongue moved to moisten her lips, which felt dry and cracked in spite of the rose lip gloss slicked over their surface. She saw his eyes follow the movement, and this time the pounding of her heart couldn't be blamed on physical exertion. He watched her tongue with a hungry intensity he couldn't disguise, any more than she could disguise the passion flaring to life inside of her.

Drew bit back a groan and sought the sweetness of her parted lips, his tongue thrusting inside her mouth to tangle with her own. Her fingers tore at the rest of the buttons on his shirt, clutching at the material until she managed to pull it away from his body. As soon as she was able to caress the soft, golden-furred surface of his chest, he jerked back from the kiss and speared her with the intensity of his bewildered gaze. "What's happening, baby? Can't you talk to me, tell me what's wrong?"

She stared up at him with passion-dazed eyes, a wild, broken note in her voice as she demanded, "Make love to me, Drew. Make love to me now!"

"First tell me what's upset you."

She tossed her head from side to side, her hair spread like a black velvet curtain over dried leaves and soft moss. "I don't want to talk," she cried out. "I want you to love me!"

"I do love you," he whispered gruffly, trailing kisses over every inch of her face. "I love you more than my own life, haven't you realized that by now? Marry me, and stay with me forever, my Gypsy."

Yes, she'd suspected the reason for his possessiveness for a very long time, she thought tiredly, she just hadn't wanted to accept it. Understanding why she'd felt increasingly stifled and trapped in their relationship didn't solve the problem, and nor did fleeing in panic from the inevitability of their parting offer a solution. She knew what she had to do, and the time had come to act on her convictions.

Inside she was screaming at the unfairness of fate, but she kept her expression free of the agony she was experiencing as she circled Drew's neck with caressing hands. "I want you," she whispered. "I want you so much."

As though he sensed the grief in store for him, his eyes darkened with emotion. "And I want you," he countered brokenly. "I want to hold you in my arms every night for the rest of our lives, and I want to give my children you as their mother. I want to cherish your body and your soul, and when we die I want to be buried in the same grave with you."

Maria recoiled inwardly, unable to stand hearing the evidence of his vulnerability. Dammit, it wasn't supposed to end this way! she thought despairingly. She'd always imagined that she would be the only one hurt when their affair came to an end. Facing the fact that Drew would suffer was more than she could bear, and she almost gave him the response he wanted from her.

Words of love trembled on her lips, until she remembered that the pain she caused him now would save him untold anguish in the future. So instead of voicing the emotion filling her heart to overflowing, she simply repeated, "Make love to me."

"Not here," he murmured. He rose abruptly and reached for her hands, pulling her to her feet in a single fluid motion. "Someone might decide to take an evening stroll, and I don't want to be interrupted when I make love to you. Tonight is too special for any distractions."

Silence reigned on the journey home, their footsteps rushed and their breathing labored. Entering

Maria's apartment, there was still no need for words. They had already been spoken, Drew's aloud and Maria's in her heart. As he picked her up and carried her into her bedroom, his face was taut with the passion he saw reflected in her eyes.

Clothing melted away as if by magic, and their moistly clinging flesh created a delicious friction that wouldn't allow for any delays. Drew entered her with a single driving thrust and she cried out in both joy and sorrow. Joy because this was truly a celebration of love, and sorrow because she was going to send him away. As she was impaled and flooded with his heat, she prayed the memory of this moment would warm her for the rest of her life.

Their joining became a poignant madness of the senses. In complete accord their movements echoed that inner frenzy, pushing them closer and closer to the edge of reason. Kiss-swollen mouths alternately demanded and pleaded, refusing to be silenced until they had both achieved a climax that ripped through them violently. With a strangled groan Drew collapsed on top of her, his chest heaving in synchronization with her own as they struggled to draw oxygen into their lungs.

Their bodies were bathed in moisture that rapidly cooled their skin, but his weight was a sweet warmth she needed in order to survive the worst coldness to come. Her arms tightened convulsively around his broad shoulders in a last outpouring of denial, and one hand rose to press his head harder against her breast.

He responded by taking her nipple into his mouth, and the magic began again. Over and over in the hours that followed they came together, until they were both drugged on the taste and feel of each other. Eventually the sun rose to spangle lacy patterns against tangled sheets, but Maria closed her eyes against the light. Because even though she clung to these final seconds of loving with all of her might, she knew the time for goodbye had finally arrived.

Fourteen

The morning sun filtered through the white mini-blinds covering the bedroom window, and sun-dappled slivers of light spread across Maria's face. She hadn't even opened her eyes when full awareness returned to her, and she wanted to lie there and weep when she remembered the reason for her depression. But this wasn't a day for weakness. She had to be strong and resolute if she hoped to convince Drew that they were through, and after the hours they'd just spent together that wasn't going to be easy.

Carefully she lifted his arm from her waist, missing its warm comfort even as she began to slide her body toward the edge of the bed. With stealthy slowness she lifted the blankets, holding her breath as her feet reached for the floor. As she stood up, she shook with an inner coldness that had little to do with the temperature of the room, and tiptoed over to the closet for something to put on.

She chose her oldest robe, needing the familiar comfort the raggedy blue velour provided. Drew had laughed at her preference, she remembered, especially when he'd threatened to buy her a new one and burn the old, and she'd reacted with outraged indignation. The memory deepened the sheen in her eyes, and she blinked rapidly to prevent her tears from falling.

After using the hall bathroom to brush her teeth and restore some order to her tangled hair, she walked into the kitchen and prepared her coffee maker. She listened to the drops sizzle against the glass carafe as she stared out the window over the sink, her mind carefully blank as she struggled to control the emotions threatening to tear her apart. When the sound of bare feet slapping against tile reached her ears, she stiffened and gripped the edge of the sink.

Two arms wrapped themselves around her waist, and a voice husky with sleep murmured against her neck. "It's cold in that bed without you. Why don't you come back and keep me from getting pneumonia, sweet thing?"

She closed her eyes as his open mouth tasted the softness of her skin, forcing a coldness into her voice that caused his entire body to tense. "I'd rather not."

His head lifted with a slowness that pointed to his confusion. "Would you like to tell me what's wrong?" he asked carefully.

"Last night was wrong."

Forcing her eyes open as she uttered the lie, she shrugged away from him and reached into the cupboard for a cup. "Would you like some coffee?" she asked in neutral tones.

Drew ignored the question, as she'd known he would. "What do you mean, last night was wrong? What are you talking about?"

"I can't marry you, Drew." Maria heard the words but couldn't believe she'd spoken them. She had felt her mouth move and her throat vibrate with the sounds she'd made, and yet her heart denied the statement so violently that her mind refused to accept what she'd said.

Drew, too, refused to accept it. "Are you crazy? Of course you can. If you're worried about giving up your career, I don't mind moving up here and ..."

"I'm worried about giving up my independence."

He leaned his side against the counter, his stare unwavering as he crossed his arms over his chest. "I'm not buying it, Maria. You love me, and I want to know what's really at the bottom of this decision."

She glanced at him briefly and continued to fill her cup with coffee. He had slipped into the slacks and shirt he'd been wearing last night, but the shirt was unbuttoned and hung loosely around his hips. He looked sleep tousled and deliciously rumpled and so beloved she wanted to jump out of the window before she said the words quivering on the tip of her tongue.

Desperate to put an end to this torture, she mentally braced herself for what she had to do. Replacing the pot on its heating element, she said, "But I don't love you, Drew."

He flinched at the admission, his eyes narrowing in suspicion as he gazed at her pale face. "I don't believe you!"

Feigning indifference, she shrugged. "I thought what I felt for you was real and lasting, but I was wrong. I guess I was confused by the physical side of our relationship. You are an exceptional lover, and I've been pretty enraptured by the way you've made me feel in bed."

An expression of horror crossed his features, and his voice was harsh with accusation. "Are you saying it was only sex between us?"

"What do you want me to say?" she asked.

Her own voice was tight with the tears she longed to shed, and its added roughness lent credence to her next remark. "I'm certain you don't want me to pretend to emotions I don't feel."

"You sure felt them last night," he countered with an ugly laugh.

"We can't spend all our time in bed," she blurted before he had time to say anything more. "I hate doing this to you, but I have no choice. Our relationship has been based on little more than the schoolgirl crush I had on you when I was younger, and now that I realize the truth I'm trying to do what's right for both of us. I don't want to see you again, Drew."

By then his face had fully hardened into a mask of rage, but he had one last question for her. "Did you suddenly figure all of this out," he asked viciously, "or have you been out for revenge all along?"

She was sickened by the conclusion he'd drawn but stood her ground. "You're wrong, but I don't expect you to believe me."

"Hardly!"

His cynical laughter held an edge of anguish, and she quickly averted her eyes from his face. But she couldn't prevent her ears from hearing or her soul from cringing at the disgust she heard in his voice. "The timing seems pretty damn convenient, since your soul-searching didn't materialize until after I spilled my guts to you," he ground out bitterly. "God! How you must have been laughing last night when I mouthed all that sentimental drivel about growing old together."

Horrified to have such a beautiful admission of love derided so cruelly, she gasped, "No, I..."

But he left the kitchen before she could complete the denial. She heard him storm down the hall and knew he was collecting the rest of his things from her bedroom. She didn't move...couldn't move. Eventually his shoes thudded against the tile of her entryway, and the front door was opened and slammed shut. She tasted the moisture trickling down her cheeks, and her steps were slow and hesitant as she wandered into the living room. There on the floor was the key ring she'd given him, and she knelt on the carpet and sobbed for all the tomorrows they would never share.

When Maria heard the pounding on her front door, she pulled a white toweling robe over her still-damp body and rushed out of the bathroom where she'd just finished showering. Pausing in the entry hall, she felt herself stiffen in dread anticipation. She knew who was on the other side of that wooden panel even before she recognized the impatient voice calling her name. "Maria, open up before I break this thing down!"

She moved closer to the door, her entire body shaking. "You gave me back your keys. I... how did you get into the main building?"

Immediately realizing how idiotic such an insignificant question sounded, her voice rose another decibel, nearly reaching hysterical levels. "It doesn't matter. Just go away, Drew. I don't want to see you."

Another series of thuds caused the door to shudder on its hinges, and she wrapped the single garment she wore closer about her shivering body. "I knew paging you wouldn't get me anywhere, so I had Charlie buzz me inside. He's a damn sight more reasonable than you, that's for certain. But I can be just as bullheaded as you, Maria. Now open this door!"

Screeching at him wasn't getting her anywhere, and if he disturbed her neighbors his actions might just get him arrested. Knowing Drew as well as she did, she faced the fact that he was unlikely to calmly depart until he'd gotten what he'd come for. Wondering just what it was he wanted with her made her cringe inwardly and hesitate before reaching out to release the bolt lock.

Instantly the knob was twisted from the outside, and she leaped back as the door flew inward. Trying desperately to generate even a small measure of courage, she demanded, "What in the world do you think you're doing, coming here at this time of night? Or at all, for that matter. I thought I told you I didn't want..."

"But I do want, Gypsy," he remarked softly, leaning against the closed door as he looked her over from the top of her steam-dampened hair to the tips of her bare toes. "I want so badly I can't eat or sleep. I want until I can't dull the ache in my body no matter how hard I try. I want until I—"

"Don't...please!"

Futilely twisting her hands together at her waist, her voice gave out on her. Her mouth opened, but no sound emerged. The longing in his eyes was reflected in hers, and she breathed deeply in an attempt to control her shattered nerves. After long, tension-fraught minutes she asked, "What point is there in rehashing everything all over again, Drew? Why can't you just accept the fact that we're through?"

Maria turned wearily, her movements as slow and halting as that of a woman three times her age. That was how she felt, she realized, since she'd convinced Drew that she didn't love him and never would. Each day was spent in an endless round of activity, going through the motions while she pretended she was still alive.

Drew followed her through the living room and into the kitchen, his eyes studying her with angry intensity. "You look like hell."

She shrugged her shoulders and reached into the cupboard over the kitchen counter. Withdrawing a glass, she filled it with water from the faucet and tipped back her head to drink thirstily. After returning the glass to the counter, she turned her head and surveyed him with a lackluster gaze. "Thank you," she responded dully. "Now that you've gotten that little barb out of the way, would you like to tell me why you're here? I thought you were still vacationing at Tricia and Marc's cabin in Pescadero."

"I got back a couple of hours ago, and not a moment too soon from the looks of things."

"I don't know what you mean."

All of the anger disappeared from his face as he walked toward her and brushed a knuckle under first one dark-rimmed eye and then the other. "What have you been doing to yourself, sweet thing?"

She winced at the endearment, wondering how he could call her that after what she'd done to him. Drawing in a trembling breath, she said, "I've been ill."

"Is that why you've lost so much weight?"

"A few pounds, which I needed to lose." Uttering a laugh that sounded strained even to her own ears, she added, "The stomach flu will do that to you."

He shook his head, shifting his hands into the pockets of the gray slacks he wore. "Not according to Tricia."

Stiffening in alarm, she asked, "What has she been telling you?"

"Only that your illness started about the time I left town. Did it, Maria?"

She quickly stared out of the window over her sink, her cheeks turning a deep rouge. "It could have. I don't really remember when I got sick."

"Tricia's very worried about you, you know."

Her expression softened, but all she managed to say was, "I know she is, but there's nothing for her to be concerned about."

"Isn't there?" he asked softly.

Gripping the edge of the tile counter in front of her, she closed her eyes rather than look at the man standing beside her. The sight of him after all these endless weeks was filling her with the anguish of her loss. She wanted to burrow into his arms and plead with him not to leave her again, even though she had been the one to send him away. Oh, God, she'd never wanted to hurt him. She would rather have died than cause him an instant of pain.

"I know you didn't mean to hurt me, honey."

Her head jerked upward, blood rushing into her cheeks as she realized she'd spoken her thoughts aloud. Yet when he reached out to touch her, her retreat was instinctively self-protective. "Please, I..."

Drew shook his head in reproof, and she remained utterly still as his hands completed their journey. Tenderly clasping her shoulders, he asked, "Why did you really send me away?"

"Because it was best for you."

His gaze solemn, he murmured, "And was it best for you, Gypsy?"

The nickname she'd grown to love was the final straw, and she slumped in defeat as she choked, "No!" Tears overflowed, bleeding from her eyes in an endless torrent. "Oh, no, Drew!"

"Then why?" he asked again.

"I had to end things before..."

Drew pulled her closer, his eyes searching her face. "You mean before I discovered the truth, don't you?"

As wary as an animal sensing a hunter, she whispered, "What are you talking about?"

"Tricia did more than just cry all over me this evening."

Instantly her face whitened. "She promised me she would never betray my confidence," she cried. "She promised me!"

Drew gave her a little shake. "And she kept her promise," he reassured her huskily. "But she also made me promise to come over here, and not leave until you'd told me how you met Thomas Phelps."

"I already told you," she whispered. "I was living on the streets, and he—"

"He took you home with him," he interrupted. "But how did you actually meet him?"

"You have no right to dredge up my past, Drew."

His eyes flashed as he sighed in exasperation. "Then to hell with explanations!"

Without another word he brushed past her, striding out of the kitchen and through the living room. She ran after him and followed him down the hall and into her bedroom. Quickly he went to the closet, pulled a suitcase down from the upper shelf and dropped it casually onto the foot of her bed. "What are you doing?" she gasped, following him as he moved toward her dresser.

"What does it look like?" he responded calmly. "I'm packing a suitcase for you."

Bolstered by a welcome surge of anger, she snapped, "And just where am I going?"

"Reno."

He grabbed a pile of undies from her top dresser drawer and gave her a triumphant smile as he easily fended off her grappling hands. "We can have a formal church ceremony later, but for now all I want to do is get the job done as quickly as possible."

Dropping her underwear onto the bed, he unzipped the brown leather case and began to shove the minute pieces of silk and lace inside. Once again she reached out to stop him, but he easily fielded her with a brawny arm. Glancing at her over his shoulder, he mocked, "What are you planning to wear for our wedding, darling?"

Shocked into utter stillness, she gaped at him. "We're not getting married."

"Oh, yes, we are," he corrected her gently, "and I suggest you hurry and get a move on. It's my guess that you aren't wearing a stitch under that robe, and I'm not in the mood to wait any longer than I have to for you. I'll carry you out of here half-naked if I have to."

"But you can't . . . we can't . . ."

"I can and we will."

"Drew, you don't understand. I can't marry you. . .I just c-can't."

"But you want to, don't you?" he asked.

When she refused to answer, his voice lost its softness, and there was a distinct warning in his next statement. "No more lies or evasions, Maria. Either you tell me why you can't marry me, or I drag you out of here kicking and screaming if I must."

Suddenly she was so tired of fighting, herself as well as him, and her shoulders slumped revealingly as she lowered herself to sit on the edge of her bed. "All right," she responded dully.

Drew moved the disordered suitcase to the floor and reached for her hand as he sat beside her. Gently rubbing the soft skin on the inside of her wrist with his thumb, he asked, "Now tell me about Tom Phelps, honey."

Maria flinched at his request, her cheeks growing paler as each second passed. She remembered the sound of sirens and flashing lights, and the almost bored voice of the police officer as he read her and the others with her their rights. She remembered the long ride downtown in the patrol car, and the horror she felt as she was fingerprinted and booked. She remembered standing before a judge, with Tom and the lawyer he'd gotten for her by her side.

Her eyes closed in an attempt to fight back the memories, but this time she failed to hold the shadow demons at bay. They came at her with rending claws that sliced new wounds over those already healed over, and the breath shuddered from her lungs in a despairing flood. As always when she recalled those hours in her past, she felt dirty and tears seeped beneath her closed eyelids and trickled down her cheeks.

"I was arrested for breaking and entering, and for theft," she admitted in a voice filled with self-loathing.

But far from sounding shocked or disgusted, Drew asked quietly, "How did that come about?"

"Through stupidity," she said harshly. "A girl-friend of mine had gone to beg for money in a shopping center parking lot. It was located in a well-to-do residential neighborhood, and on her way back she saw a family loading luggage into their car. After they drove away, she hurried back to tell the rest of us and to suggest we use the house while the owners were away for the weekend."

She shook her head, and her lips twisted cynically. "Since we were hiding out in an old warehouse with a leaky roof at the time, and it was pouring like crazy outside, she didn't have to do much convincing."

"Where did the theft come in?" he asked. "You're honest to your soul, Maria. You might have broken into someone's house to find comfortable shelter, but you wouldn't have stolen from them."

She looked at him and smiled. "You didn't know me then," she stated bluntly. "I'd been on the streets for over a year, and I was pretty hard-nosed by that time. I'd stolen before, food mostly, but I'd never gotten caught. That weekend my luck ran out.

"I only knew that one girl and her boyfriend really well," she continued after a moment. "They were both a couple of years younger than me, but the other guy that came with us was a lot older and had hitched into California from another state. We didn't know too much about him, but there's an unwritten code on the streets. You stick together and help each other out, so when he started using the warehouse as a base the rest of us didn't have much to say about it. It wasn't until the neighbors called the police and they found some jewelry stashed in his bag that we realized he hadn't just been using the bathroom when he disappeared for a while.''

Drew looked grim at her admission, but there was the softness of pity in his eyes. "And Tom was one of the cops that arrested you?''

"No, he was the booking officer,'' she corrected with a shake of her head. "When he questioned me he was kinder than I deserved, and I leveled with him. Later he hired a good lawyer to defend me and my friends. We were all convicted of breaking and entering, but only the older guy who'd stolen the jewelry went to jail. Since none of us had a prior criminal record the judge went light on us. My friends were sent to a youth rehabilitation camp, and I was released with a suspended sentence.''

"And you went to live with Tom,'' he stated with a smile.

"Yes,'' she replied simply. "By that time I trusted him, and he was as alone as I was. Once I asked him why he had ever believed me in the first place, and he told me it was something he'd seen in my eyes that night, an expression of hopelessness he'd only seen in the very old or the most despondent.''

"I can imagine," Drew murmured, squeezing her hand, "but I don't see what this has to do with you not being willing to marry me, sweetheart."

As though a single sentence would explain her stand, she said, "I was eighteen."

He frowned in perplexity. "You were still very young. Don't you think it's time to forgive yourself for what happened, and get on with your life?"

With impatience borne of frustration, she jerked her hand away from his and shook her head in a violently negative gesture. "For heaven's sake you're a lawyer, Drew. I was tried as an adult, and as a result I'll always have a criminal record. If you married me you would be throwing away your good name, and any hopes you might have for a political career."

"So that's it!"

He exhaled explosively and immediately uttered a relieved laugh. "You little fool, if I wanted a political career I'd still be in Washington. I took up that appointment to see if I was geared in that direction and to please my father. I wasn't. I'm perfectly satisfied with being a defense attorney."

"You might change your mind, and even if you didn't, my past could only harm you."

"Then we'll deflect any potential weapons by being up-front with the media. By the time we're finished constructing your press release, you'll be considered a heroine and a sterling example to all the lost, disturbed kids who find themselves in trouble. And as far as I'm concerned," he concluded firmly, "I'll never be anything but proud of my wife."

Maria lifted her head to look at him, her voice trembling. "Do you mean that?"

"With all my heart," he replied gruffly.

His lips formed a curve so sweet she ached to trace it with her fingers, but deliberately resisted the temptation. "Drew...you don't know everything yet."

He bent his head and began kissing her neck. "Mmm, there's more?"

She gasped and closed her eyes as warmth flooded through her. "I...there's my background. You know I was orphaned, but not the circumstances. Drew, my mother was admitted to Fairmont County Hospital in the last stages of labor. No one knew who she was and she carried no identification. She was assumed to be an illegal alien from Mexico, which was why the hospital staff named me Maria, but I can't even be certain of that. Without a nationality, any children I have would be denied half of their heritage."

"Your parents must have been exceptional people to have given birth to a daughter like you, and our children will be blessed to have you as their mother."

At this declaration her eyes widened in wonder, and she began to cry. "I love you," she whispered brokenly. "I love you so much, but I'm so afraid."

"You never have to be afraid again," he reassured her gently, his eyes alight with the strength of his emotions.

Framing her face with his hands, he bore her back on the bed and leaned over her. His mouth tenderly traced her moist cheeks, absorbing her tears and making them a part of him. "I'll always love and protect you, my Gypsy. I love you for the strong, courageous woman you are, just as I love you for the rebellious, frightened child you were. That kind of love is a miracle, sweetheart, and miracles shouldn't be wasted."

His mouth pressed down on hers with hungry urgency, and for long moments only the sound of their mingled sighs and moans filled the room. Then he lifted his head, his silver eyes glowing with a depth of emotion that warmed them both. "You'll marry me?" he questioned, parting the edges of her robe with a hand that shook visibly.

As his fingers began to trace the yielding softness of her body, Maria studied his beloved features with a sense of awe. She wondered if the sky outside was bathed in the glow of a lover's moon, and knew it didn't really matter. Once she'd needed that gentle radiance to see her way past the shadows lurking in the darkness, but now Drew's love and acceptance had guided her into the light. She was home and safe in his arms. There really were miracles, she thought joyously, wrapping her arms around the man she adored. There really were....

*   *   *   *   *

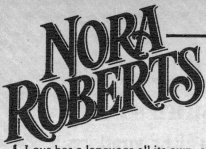

NORA ROBERTS

Love has a language all its own, and for centuries, flowers have symbolized love's finest expression. Discover the language of flowers—and love—in this romantic collection of 48 favorite books by bestselling author Nora Roberts.

Starting in February, two titles will be available each month at your favorite retail outlet.

In February, look for:

Irish Thoroughbred, **Volume #1**
The Law Is A Lady, **Volume #2**

In March, look for:

Irish Rose, **Volume #3**
Storm Warning, **Volume #4**

Collect all 48 titles and become fluent in

THE LANGUAGE OF LOVE

Take 4 bestselling love stories FREE
Plus get a FREE surprise gift!

Coming in February from

THE BLACK SHEEP
by Laura Leone

Man of the Month Roe Hunter
wanted nothing to do with
free-spirited Gingie Potter.

Yet beneath her funky fashions
was a woman's heart—and body—
he couldn't ignore.

You met Gingie in
Silhouette Desire #507
A WILDER NAME
also by Laura Leone
Now she's back.

SDBL

The Case of the
Mesmerizing Boss
DIANA PALMER

Diana Palmer's exciting new series,
MOST WANTED, begins in March with
THE CASE OF THE MESMERIZING BOSS....

Dane Lassiter—one-time Texas Ranger
extraordinaire—now heads his own group of
crack private detectives. Soul-scarred by
women, this heart-stopping private eyeful
exists only for his work—until the night his
secretary, Tess Meriwether, becomes the target
of drug dealers. Dane wants to keep her safe.
But their stormy past makes him the one man
Tess *doesn't* want protecting her....

Don't miss THE CASE OF THE MESMERIZING
BOSS by Diana Palmer, first in a lineup of
heroes MOST WANTED! In June, watch for THE
CASE OF THE CONFIRMED BACHELOR...only
from Silhouette Desire!

SDDP-1

MOST WANTED